FRONT
AND
CENTER

FRONT AND CENTER

by
Catherine Gilbert Murdock

Houghton Mifflin
HOUGHTON MIFFLIN HARCOURT
BOSTON   NEW YORK   2009

Houghton Mifflin is an imprint of Houghton Mifflin Harcourt Publishing Company.

www.hmhbooks.com

The text of this book is set in Dante MT.

Library of Congress Cataloging-in-Publication Data is on file.
ISBN 978-0-618-95982-2

Manufactured in the United States of America
MV 10 9 8 7 6 5 4 3 2 1

To Viviana, who made this possible

CONTENTS

FRONT
AND
CENTER

1
BACK TO SCHOOL

HERE ARE TEN WORDS I NEVER thought I'd be saying . . .
Well, okay, sure. I say these words all the time. It's not like
school and *good* and *to* are the kind of words you can avoid
even if you wanted to. It's just that I've never said them in this
particular order. Not that I can remember, anyway. But what
do you know, there they were inside my head, like a little
thing you'd say just to get yourself psyched: *It sure feels good to
be going back to school.*

Because you know what? It did. It felt really good, actually,
even though school hasn't exactly ever been the center of my
happiness. Normally it's kind of the opposite, a huge boring
thing I have to put up with while I'm waiting for practice
to start. Or a game, if it happens to be a game day, when
the clocks go fifty times slower than they normally do and
you can't hear a word the teacher says, your head's so on
the court already. But today I was actually looking forward
to it all, actually looking forward to the classes and the teachers and even those stupid crackly announcements. Because

today, after five months of sheer absolute insanity, my life was finally getting back to normal.

No more football: that was one good thing. The season was over at last, so now I didn't have to worry about everyone in the state of Wisconsin jawing about how weird it was for a girl to be playing, and then jawing about how terrible and awful and un-team-spirit-like it was for me to quit even though I wasn't *quitting*, I was just saving my shoulder, which you'd think no one had ever heard of before, a player leaving because of an injury. But now hoops season was starting up, which is what I'd been saving my shoulder *for*, for basketball, and no one would jaw about me for even a second except to say stuff like "Nice shot" or "When's your next game?" which is the kind of jawing I've been hearing forever and don't mind at all. So that was one good thing.

Plus I was home at last. At the moment I was driving to school, duh, but officially I was at home instead of at a huge shiny hospital, trying to convince my oldest brother not to kill himself, and then once he got his spirit back trying to convince him not to kill *me* because he was so desperate to boss someone around. Now Mom got to be that victim, which she was actually happy about because she's a mom, and instead I got to live in our beat-up old house, eating real home-cooked food if you call what Dad makes food, and drive our beat-up old Caravan, and that was totally A-okay with me. Even the cooking.

But most of all — and this is what I was looking forward to the very, very most — I was done with all that *boyfriend* crap. Finished with the 24/7 Brian Nelson cable station that had been running nonstop inside my skull since July. No more feeling like I was some fluttery girl who doesn't have anything better to do all day long than think about her *boyfriend*. Because I did have better things to think about, thank you very much, because I am not the kind of girl who has boyfriends; I'm the kind who's just friends with boys, which is totally different and which I'm actually kind of good at. I'd pulled the plug on that Brian Nelson cable station for good.

That's why it felt so nice to be getting back to school. Because after five months I was back to being plain old background D.J. That's how I thought about it, anyway. In photographs of course I'm always in the background — it's a family joke that us Schwenk kids could go to school naked on picture day because we're all so crazy tall. But I mean that I was returning to the background of life. Where no one would really notice me or talk about me or even talk *to* me much except to say "Nice shot," and I could just hang out without too many worries at all.

Anyway, the words *normal* and *background* and *basketball* were kind of percolating through my brain — kind of the way water glugs in those big coffeepots they rev up after church, although without that coffee smell — as I drove along with Curtis.

"So," I said, feeling normal and happy enough to take a stab at a real normal conversation.

Curtis flinched, sitting there next to me. There are rabbits, wild rabbits, calmer than my little brother, the way he acts sometimes. Then he hunkered down in his seat. "Sorry," he mumbled.

"It's okay. I was just wondering how Sarah's doing."

Again: making conversation. Not even using the word *girlfriend*. But Curtis's ears turned red like I'd asked him to walk through town in his underwear.

"I mean, maybe you could have her over sometime. For supper or something."

Which made Curtis go even redder. He hunkered down further and started picking at his jeans like they were so fascinating that no one could possibly be interested in anything else. "Yeah. Maybe." He didn't say anything else either, for the rest of the ride. Not one word.

So much for making conversation.

I pulled up to the middle school. Curtis heaved up his backpack, heavy even for him. "See you," he said, because Mom taught him that one little bit of manners at least.

"Five-thirty, right?"

He nodded. Then, his legs already out of the Caravan, he turned back. "So, I was wondering how Brian was. Maybe you could have him over for supper."

My jaw dropped. Literally. I could not *believe* he said that.

Of all the mean, thoughtless . . . And then I saw his mouth twitch and I finally got it: he was teasing me.

I lunged at him but the seat belt caught me, and then he was out of the Caravan, grinning like a maniac and hustling into the building with a crowd of kids half his size.

What a total little — I mean, here's a kid who talks less than a *rock,* and it turns out the whole ride he'd been planning how to bounce back what I'd said. If it was anyone else rubbing it in about Brian, that would be one thing. But Curtis — that's like getting mad at your dog. Although if Curtis kept pulling stunts like that, maybe I'd have to stop thinking of him as some poor little house pet and start thinking of him as a smart-mouthed kid who maybe needed a lesson on respect.

At least I was prepared for all the questions about Win. In just the few days I'd been home, wandering around town after Thanksgiving, I'd learned that pretty much every single person in Red Bend considered it their personal duty to grill me on how he was doing every single time they saw me. Once on Saturday I let on that I was getting really tired of having to repeat this conversation, and old Mrs. Ingalls looked so upset that I felt twice as bad about hurting her feelings as she probably did about Win. That's when I learned just to say, "He's doing okay, thanks," and leave it at that.

That's how it went in school, too, practically every kid

asking, "How's Win?" Or "Is he walking yet?" because everyone has this huge hang-up about walking, like it's the most important thing you can do after you break your neck. And every time I'd answer, "He's getting there" or "He's working hard," instead of saying that these days Win was working mostly on feeding himself and that maybe in the big picture of life being able to eat without assistance is a lot more important than managing a few little steps. I sure thought it, though.

I had to check in at the main office first thing, turn in these forms showing I'd been absent twenty-seven days on purpose and not because I'm a juvenile delinquent. Mrs. Henning asked about Win of course, and was telling me that if there was anything we needed just let her know, like I would obviously think of her first, when there was this huge yell of "Geronimo!" and I had enough sense to brace my feet just as Beaner leapt up onto my back.

Beaner Halstaad is as skinny as a string bean and has more energy than a jumping bean. He'd started doing this jump-on-my-back thing during football, and I guess he hadn't gotten tired of it yet. Right away he started pounding on my shoulders. "You're back, dude! That's so awesome! Check it out, Mrs. Henning. She's back! Isn't that awesome?"

"Hello, Beaner," said Mrs. Henning, like his behavior was completely normal. Which for Beaner it is.

"Hey, guess what?" Beaner poked me. "I told Justin Hunsberger you were going to be playing boys' basketball!"

Even Mrs. Henning had to smile at that one.

"What'd he say?" I asked. Because of course Justin Huns-berger hates my guts like nobody's business. And totally vice versa, too.

"Oh, man, it was awesome." Beaner jumped down. "He was like, 'No way, no *way*,' and I was totally serious, saying all this stuff about how you'd found this loophole and really needed to grab recruiters because of missing last season and everything. And he totally bought it! You should've seen his face!"

Mrs. Henning went back to her desk with this smile like *Kids today*, and I couldn't help laughing with Beaner.

"Maybe I should suit up for it," I said.

"Oh, man, wouldn't that be awesome! He'd have a to-tal cow!"

"Tell him we're running screens." I cracked up at the thought of Justin's face when he thought I'd be knocking him down on purpose.

"Oh, *man* . . . You gotta show up, just for today! C'mon, it would so totally rock! Hey, by the way, my folks are having this thing, you know, after the game Friday, for all the players and their parents, the guy players. You want to come?"

"All the *guy* players?"

"Hey, cut me some slack." He grinned. "It'll be cool. I gotta go." He dashed out the door like he'd keel over dead if he slowed down for just a second. Then he dashed back in: "And check out your locker!"

"My *locker?*" But he was already gone.

So, seeing as it looked like I was done with Mrs. Henning and her D.J.-is-not-a-juvenile-delinquent forms, I headed that way. Which I would have done anyway, of course, only now I was worried. I mean, I hadn't checked it in more than a month. I didn't think I'd left any food in there, but you never know.

I kept my head down on the way there, trying to duck the Win questions, though once when I looked up I did notice a locker decked out in wrapping paper and balloons like it was a giant birthday present or something, done up the way the popular girls, the cheerleaders especially, do each other's lockers sometimes.

Then I did a double take, because it was *my* locker that was all done up. And people were pointing at it, grinning at each other, and a couple kids were staring at the pictures stuck all over the front, although as soon as they saw me coming the kids slunk away.

I know all about the stuff done to lockers. Just a few months ago my best friend's locker got trashed because some kids get a kick out of picking on kids who are a little bit different. And even though part of my brain was pointing out that it wasn't graffiti, I still panicked. Because even though the gift wrap *looked* nice, who knew how mean it'd actually *be?*

But here's the thing: it really was gift wrap. Friendly gift wrap, not Happy Birthday or anything like that, or Welcome

Baby! which Mom had to use for Christmas one year because we'd run out of Christmas wrapping paper and it was too late to buy more. And taped on top was a big sign that said WELCOME BACK! WE MISSED YOU! signed by all the girls on the basketball team.

Other things were taped up as well, like a picture of me from last year before I had to quit the team, and basketball stickers. And right in the middle — maybe that's why those kids had been staring — was a copy of that photograph of me from *People* magazine where I'm dribbling in to shoot and Brian has his arm around my waist. Which hadn't been the best way to announce to the universe that Red Bend's girl linebacker and the quarterback of our eternal archrival were kind of involved. Just looking at it now, my ears got hot. But someone — probably Kari Jorgensen, she's so creative — had cut Brian out of the picture so it was just me, and then over my body where Brian's arm had been she'd made a perfect little T-shirt out of paper and colored it in with my number 12, with "Red Bend" printed on it and everything. It was nicer looking than our real uniforms.

Then *that* whole photo of me in my paper 12 jersey was stuck on top of *another* piece of paper — how long had this taken? — with just-as-nice lettering that said D.J. IS #1!!! Which when you think of it is a little dumb, because right below is me wearing #12. And D.J. IS #1!! was on the balloons too.

Well. I stood there just staring, wondering how long they'd been planning this, probably coming in way early with the custodians to have it ready for me, girls like Kari who had so much important stuff to do and are pretty popular, not to mention just plain pretty. All that effort for me. No one had ever decorated a locker for me before. No one had ever singled me out like this, with pictures and balloons and announcements to the world that I'm number one.

And then who should show up but Justin Hunsberger.

"Hey," he said. Which usually isn't insulting, but it sounds really different coming from him.

"Hey," I said back, just as cold. Now what was I supposed to say? *Sorry I missed the rest of football season just because I had to save my shoulder and my brother? Sorry for even trying out considering how you whined about me to anyone who would listen until pretty much the day I left?* No, I don't think so. Sorry's out.

Justin kicked at the floor. He was wearing a Red Bend Football T-shirt in case someone in the building by some freak of ignorance still didn't know he played. "Hey," he said again. "Your brother —"

"He's not walking yet. But thanks for asking." Although I sure didn't sound thankful.

"No, that's not . . . It's just . . ." He looked up. "I'm praying for him, okay? I pray for him every day. He's . . . he's a really amazing guy." He kicked the floor. "That's all."

I swallowed. "Oh."

"Yeah. So. See you around."

"Yeah," I said, wishing I had some idea what in the *world* to say other than that I actually wouldn't be playing boys' basketball, which I didn't think had quite, you know, the right tone at this particular moment. But of course I couldn't think of a thing.

Justin nodded and headed down the hall.

Of course then I thought of something. "I'll tell him!" I called out. But I'm not sure Justin even heard me.

I was still staring after him, wondering what the heck had just happened, when out of nowhere Beaner showed up again. This time at least he didn't jump on me. He just put his arm around my shoulders in his buddy way.

"Pretty awesome, huh?" he asked, studying my locker.

"What? Um, yeah. It is."

"So you coming?" He squeezed my shoulder.

"To what?"

"To my *party.*" He sighed this huge sigh. "I can't believe you forgot *already.* The parental units? Post-game? You're coming?"

"Beaner! You just asked. Give me a bit of time here."

He looked at the ceiling and whistled to himself. "Okay . . . Was that time enough?"

Now he had me laughing. "No! This is my first day back — I'll have a ton of homework —"

"Homework, schmomework. This is a *date,* girlfriend."

"A date?" I grinned at the joke, even though he wasn't grinning that way.

"You betcha . . . Hey, my man! Wait up!" And with that he zoomed away.

A *date?* Like — like what people in the movies do? What was he talking about?

"Hey!" Beaner shouted. Far down the hall, he was holding himself up on two guys' shoulders. "Don't blow me off now! This is a *date,* you know!" Then he shot me a pretend lay-up and disappeared into the crowd.

Everyone — *everyone* — in the hall heard him. Maybe everyone in the whole school. And every single one of them turned and looked straight at me.

Double quick I spun away, my face burning five kinds of fire, and made a big project of opening my locker.

Which was just wonderful considering I hadn't been all that confident about the combination before this, and Beaner's little announcement sure didn't help any.

I got it open, finally. The good news is that nothing smelled. It was just snapshots of Win and Curtis and Bill, and our good dog Smut with the slimy football she carries everywhere, and books I could have used in Minneapolis, and an old Red Bend Basketball sweatshirt that wasn't even dirty.

I should have been relieved, but I didn't feel relief at all. Well, I was a little relieved my locker didn't smell like a lab experiment. And it was nice to see those pictures I like so much, and my favorite sweatshirt, after six straight weeks of not seeing them once. But it wasn't enough. Four snapshots and a sweatshirt weren't nearly enough to balance out all this other weirdness.

By which I mean: How are you supposed to hate a guy who prays for your family? How mind-blowing, how totally mind-blowing, is that?

Not to mention the whole locker business. Don't get me wrong: it was super nice of the team to spend all that time making my locker look like a homecoming parade. I should have been totally, 100% grateful. But now all around me I could hear kids laughing and whispering about it. About me. And now everyone would know where my locker was, and maybe even think about it — think about *me* — whenever they passed. Sure, I was stoked to be back for hoops season, and I know I'm a pretty big part of the team. But I'd never in a million years want anyone thinking I *expected* this sort of number-one treatment; that's the last thing I wanted. I just wanted, you know, to play. The girls should have saved their wrapping paper and balloons and all their enthusiasm for someone else. Someone who didn't want to trade it for a boring old anonymous life.

Speaking of which, it's also pretty hard to have a boring old anonymous life when your best guy friend in school decides to announce the two of you have a date. Which I'm not even going to get started on except to say *WHAT THE HECK*

WAS BEANER THINKING? Meaning what was he thinking to be saying that in front of two hundred kids, *and* what was he thinking about us even dating, whatever a date with Beaner even means?

That's the thing. When I said that it sure felt good to be going back to school, I didn't mean just going to *school*. I meant having everything go back to the way it used to be. The way it's always been. With D.J. Schwenk in the background, just like always. In the background where I belong.

But instead, it was the exact total opposite. Instead of being a nobody, now I was front and center.

And let me tell you something. Front and center sucks.

2
D.J. Schwenk Is #1!!

IF YOU DON'T KNOW BASKETBALL, you probably don't think too much about positions. I mean, I'm sure it looks pretty crazy out there sometimes, players running around everywhere all over the court. And really, it's every player's job to score and defend and pass, and put that way positions don't matter a lot. But there *are* positions in hoops, even if they're not obvious. And just like the quarterback is the most important position in football because he holds the ball and calls the plays, the most important player in basketball is the point guard. More important even, because point guard plays both offense and defense the way a QB doesn't, and calls plays continually, changing strategy and directing the four other players almost like a coach, because of course the coach can't be out on the floor. And just like *quarterback* gets shortened to *QB*, at some point folks started calling the basketball positions by numbers instead. Like small forward is three, and center is five. And point guard is number one.

Which is why I was so freaked about my locker even after it was clear that it wasn't mean or anything. Because all those

#1 signs — even though I'm sure the girls didn't mean it this way — they were bringing up, yet again, that I should be playing point.

Ever since grade school it's been obvious that I have the potential to be a pretty good point guard. I've got the ball skills, after all, and I know my way around the court like nobody's business, and both of those are really important attributes. From my very first day of practice, coaches have been nudging me that way. But then after a while — sometimes it only takes a couple of minutes — the coach will decide I'm probably better as a forward, or a center. And instead they'll play as point guard a girl who maybe can't dribble so well, and isn't such an accurate passer, and who doesn't get strategy in that automatic Schwenk way. But that girl, whoever she is and however bad she plays, is always a better number one than I am because she can do the one thing I can't. The most important thing of all for a point guard. That girl can *speak.*

Freshman year of high school, Coach K had big plans for me. Amy Hagendorf was starting at one but she was a senior, and he figured he'd have a whole season to break me in, slipping me in so I'd get a feel for the position. It didn't work. I mean, it worked when we were really far ahead so there wasn't any pressure, and once it worked when we were really far behind and everyone knew we'd never make up those seventeen points, not if we had the whole NBA playing for us.

Then I was okay. But crunch time? No way. Maybe if you stopped the clock and everyone in the gym shut their mouth and gave me a couple minutes to figure out how to express myself . . . But that's pretty much the opposite of how crunch time works. Dump that kind of pressure on background-loving D.J., and I might as well be out there with a piece of duct tape over my mouth.

Sophomore year Amy Hagendorf was gone, of course, off to UWM, and so it was all on me. Which lasted one game until Coach K decided Kari Jorgensen should play one and make the position, you know, an actual asset to the team. Which is why we beat Hawley in a total upset, because Kari played point and I played the game of my life as center, just taking the court apart and not even fouling out until the last minute of the game. There were times actually when Kari and I would sort of pair up together and I'd whisper what to do, or what to say, and then she'd get it done in a way neither of us could working alone. And then after that, well, it didn't matter anymore because I had to quit basketball because of Dad's hip.

Looking at those D.J. IS #1!! balloons now, the numbers the girls had drawn in bubble letters, I felt a little sick to my stomach. Like I said, the girls didn't intend anything mean I'm sure, but those #1 signs just reminded me of how I'd failed in the past. How many times coaches had told me I could do it, and how many times I'd proved them wrong. Now, I couldn't help but suspect, Coach K was going to try one more time. And I was going to disappoint them, Coach K and Kari and all the rest of the team. Disappoint them again.

All day long everyone asked a million questions about Win — the same million questions, over and over, until I actually thought about writing something on my forehead with a Sharpie, just to save my breath. The teachers were just as talky, asking the same questions but in a quiet, you-can-tell-*me* voice. And you could tell they were pleased I'd gotten so much homework done, and I didn't get any grief — not yet, anyway — about how maybe the quality of that homework wasn't so great. It's not like I had anyone in the rehab hospital to chat with about *Ethan Frome,* and anyway, who'd want to talk for two seconds about such a depressing book. And let's not even get started on algebra.

Mrs. LeVoir, the Spanish teacher, even said she'd have lunch with me to help me review. Which should have been nice — I mean, it *is* nice that she volunteered to give up her free time like that, make her own little contribution to the whole Schwenk Family Tragedy. But it's not like I could say, *That's okay, I'd rather flunk Spanish and let you eat your cottage cheese with the grownups.* So I just thanked her, and all the other teachers, especially Mr. Larson, who I actually really do like and who in three minutes explained small intestine membranes so that I finally understood what the anatomy textbook was talking about.

Plus Amber finally showed up.

Amber's the one who had all that awful stuff done to her locker last fall — that's how I know how bad it can get, how locker stuff can get really hurtful. It got so bad for her finally that she and Dale (which explains the meanness on some people's part, the fact she has a girlfriend) left town altogether. They'd spent a month living in Dale's truck camper, which is barely big enough to turn around in, especially for two people like Amber and Dale who aren't exactly size zero. (Did you know that zero is actually a *size*? Who the heck is a size *zero*? Do they walk around all the time saying "I fit into nothing," ha?) Then they moved in with a friend of Dale's in Chicago but apparently that place wasn't much bigger than the camper and Dale hadn't ever been too pleased about Amber dropping out of school, so when they found out I was coming back to Red Bend, they came too, and Amber more or less made up with her mother, who was as big a jerk about Dale as the biggest jerks in school, and now Amber's trying for her diploma.

Which meant Mom — my mom, who has much more important things to worry about than *sexual perversion*, which Amber's mom actually said out loud even though that's a laugh coming from her — called a bunch of school administrators, administrators other than herself, and worked it out so Amber could show up for classes and nothing else. Because she was being bullied. Which somehow ended up as Principal Slutsky lecturing me about how I should have reported it. To which Mom said, "I guess no one has been pulling their weight like they should have, wouldn't you say?" Just to make the point that Mr. Slutsky had dropped the ball last October. Sometimes, you know, Mom can really shine.

So there I was answering the eight millionth question about Win when Amber shows up still in her coat, I'm sure to rub it in to everyone that she has permission to come in late, and gives me a big hug and starts complaining about the work *she* has to make up.

To tell you the truth, if I hadn't known her so well, and Dale, who's about the coolest girl ever, that hug would have wigged me out just as much as it seemed to wig out the kids around us. There was a time over the summer when just the thought of Amber gave me the shivers, particularly seeing as we'd spent years as best friends on sleepovers and everything without me knowing about her particular, you know, preferences. But it didn't bother me so much anymore, because I was smart enough now to know it isn't disgusting when a girl who likes girls touches another girl. It's just, you know, life. Like just because a guy who likes girls touches one, it doesn't mean they're going out. Like me and Beaner . . . although now maybe that wasn't such a good example. Anyway, it sure felt nice to have my oldest friend there, complaining in a way that just cracked me up and also blocking me from all the Win questioners, because most kids weren't rude enough to interrupt, and the ones who were weren't brave enough or dumb enough to interrupt Amber.

⊚ ⊚ ⊚ ⊚

The only downer was that she wasn't playing basketball. Not with school, plus all her makeup work, plus her job at the Super Saver. Which really stinks, because Amber is an awesome defender. When she sticks herself to another player, you can just write that girl off. But no matter what I'd said, and Dale too, which was nice considering how much they need money, Amber said no. So it was a real bummer to suit up without her there in the locker room, although at least someone had stuck wrapping paper on my gym locker as well. And then once we were all out on the court, Kari got everyone going on this cheer she'd made up just for me. Even Coach K cracked a smile and said he was glad I was back.

Coach K isn't *the* Coach K — like the Duke coach commutes to Wisconsin for a bunch of girls! — because he's Kibblehouse, not Krzyzewski. But he's still Coach K to us. He teaches shop and he's very strict, which I guess you have to be if you're teaching a roomful of guys about blowtorches. He used to coach boys until his son was a freshman, but then even after his son graduated, he kept coaching girls because he says they create a team automatically. Which I guess we do. I mean, could you imagine a bunch of boys decorating each other's lockers and making up cheers? He says it's a lot easier to train a girl to shoot than it is to train a guy to pass.

You know how our football coach chews his mustache when he's thinking? Coach K always twirls a pen, a special kind of pen that comes with a chain so he won't lose it. All the way in one direction until it's wound tight around his hand, then all the way around in the other. Late in a game it's best to stay to his left if you don't want to lose an eye.

Boy, did I miss Amber. I didn't have someone to goof off with for one thing, but we also flat out needed her. Kayla Frolingsdorf and Brittany Graebel are okay — they're juniors too — and we had some underclassmen I barely remembered, but it wasn't like Amber's shoes were going to get filled by any of them. And Jessica Hudak, who's a senior with Kari, and one more senior as well: Ashley Erdel. What that girl was doing here now, as a senior, I had no idea. Ashley hadn't played hoops since middle school! Just a few minutes into practice, she was red-faced and puffing, her hair stuck to the back of her neck in dark sticky curls. She might get the best grades in Red Bend, but she had benchwarmer written all over her.

You could tell it was a huge relief to Ashley when practice ended, though I could have gone another couple days, I was enjoying it all so much. It didn't hurt that Beaner showed up right at the end, all ready for *his* basketball practice, and the two of us played one on one until his coach told me I was making the boys look bad.

Beaner is really fast, which shouldn't surprise you, and he can jump like just about anything, so when you're playing against him you have to be super alert all the time for his steals. But he's also . . . Well, if I was his coach I'd call him lazy, or cocky maybe, because half the time he stole from me I'd steal it right back, grab it when he was still hooting away. The other guys liked that a lot, I could tell. Plus whenever he went in I'd be right there in his face rebounding, which might surprise a guy who didn't know me, but Beaner doesn't get bothered one way or the other. He never treats me like I'm a girl, which means he's not too cautious but he's also not a bully either, just because the person guarding him happens to wear a bra. I've played against guys like that and you just want to dump a bucket of ice over their heads, or down their shorts, which would be more appropriate, just to get them to grow up a little. But Beaner treats me like I'm human. Which means he does everything he can to beat me and then afterward tells me how good I played, no matter who won.

"You still thinking about Friday?" he asked as he was grabbing some water.

"You still got a hoop in your driveway?" I asked.

He looked at me like I was crazy, but I couldn't keep a straight face and we both started laughing. Because hello, this is Wisconsin, where we've already had a couple feet of snow and it's not even officially winter. "I'll get it shoveled for ya," he said.

"Okay then. I'll be there." And I grinned at him and headed off to the showers.

Normally after practice I go to the library, hanging out until Curtis's practice finishes because neither the middle school or the high school has enough room for the girls and boys to practice at the same time. But Coach K was waiting by the locker room entrance when I came out, waiting like he'd been there awhile, and before I could say a word he asked if we could talk.

Every time we play an important game, Coach K puts a little tag with the opponent's name and score and the year on his pen and hangs it in his office as a souvenir. Right there in the middle was the pen from last year's Hawley game, where he got so excited that he actually snapped his pen off its chain and it went sailing onto the basketball court and Jessica stomped on it by mistake and they had to call a time-out so the refs could pick up the pieces. So now it was really easy to identify because of all the Scotch tape.

"So. Betcha you're wondering why you're here," he said, tilting back in his chair and working his latest pen, catching it in his hand every time.

"Point guard," I said. Might as well rip that Band-Aid off right away.

"I have been doing some thinking on that subject. But you know . . . I stopped by your folks' place last week, and your dad, well, he passed these along." Coach K lifted up this big shopping bag with a grunt and dumped it out onto his desk.

It was envelopes. A couple dozen at least. With fancy logos in the spot where you write who the letter's from, big capital letters that took me a few minutes to figure out were university logos. And beneath the logos, the words *Women's Basketball Program*.

And right in the middle of every envelope, above our home address, or the school address sometimes, was my name.

I finally figured it out: recruiting letters. "But — but I didn't even *play* last year!"

"Lot of folks read *People*. A girl linebacker who scores twenty points a game, well, that caught their attention."

That stupid article! A couple months ago these two guys came by our place and of course I was really nice to them, me and Brian together because we thought they were farmers, but it turned out they were really from *People* magazine come to do a story on Red Bend's girl football player. And in the article they made a huge deal out of the whole Brian thing, which was great news for him and for me both — I'm kidding, it was absolutely horrible — and no matter how much time passed, people kept bringing it up. It was like a curse, a dead hand or something from a horror movie that kept coming back no matter how many times you buried it. The photograph stuck to my locker this morning, and now here it was again.

"Why didn't Dad give me these?" I asked finally.

"You already had a lot you were dealing with there. He

didn't want to add any more pressure." Coach K sighed. "I'm afraid I dropped the ball here, D.J. We should have already been thinking, you know, about where you want to go. We should have been thinking about it last year. You have any preferences, school-wise?"

I shook my head. I just wanted to go *somewhere*. Somewhere with a scholarship, duh, that got me out of Red Bend.

"I've got some networking I can do. But no one's going to offer you anything if they don't know you're interested. The NCAA won't even let coaches call you. You've got to reach out."

"I've got to call *coaches?*" Although now I remembered Bill calling schools. How complicated it was, and how relieved everyone was when he decided on the University of Minnesota.

"You need to market yourself. You need to present yourself as a natural leader."

"I'm not a natural —"

"You're not? Look at you and Win. You took someone with a lot of promise and a lot of problems, and you got him to recognize his talents and overcome his weaknesses. You know what that is?"

Cruel? I thought. Because if Coach K had heard me yelling at Win, he probably would have locked me up.

"That's leadership. Win and Bill didn't get those scholarships just because of their athletic ability. They got them because they're hard-working natural leaders. Just like you."

I wondered if I could change the subject to something less embarrassing. Sex ed, maybe. Anything would be less embarrassing than this.

"We need to figure out how to get out all that leadership trapped inside you. How would you do it, D.J.? Let's say now that you were coach and you had this amazing girl who was too shy, you know, to say much. To speak up on the court."

I gulped. "I don't know. Maybe have her practice?"

"Practice. That's a super idea. Why dontcha think about practicing your leadership."

"Oh. Okay." Not asking, *When is this wonderful conversation going to end?*

"You understand why, dontcha? You need to show these schools what you're capable of. Anyone can sink a ball — Sasha Christensen could sink a ball. But leadership . . . that's something special. That's something any school would pay for. Pay a lot."

By now I was seriously panicking — not so you could tell, but my guts were pretty much sausage. Sasha Christensen had played back when I was in eighth grade, the most famous girl player in Red Bend. She'd ended up getting a full scholarship to Michigan State. I'd gone to every one of her games I could — I mean, she was *amazing*. "Couldn't we wait? My mom's not even home right now. And I'm only a junior . . ."

Coach K fiddled with his pen. "That's the thing. That coach from the University of Minnesota? The one you talked to last month? She called me this morning."

"Called *you?*"

"She wanted me to give you a heads-up that another girl committed — committed verbally. So they only have one scholarship left."

"Oh. But I'm not going to college next year."

"You don't understand." He looked at me like this was really important. After I heard his next bit, I knew why. "They only have one scholarship left for *your* year. For juniors. That's the thing. These kids verbal so early that if you don't get out there, *right now* . . . even if a school wants you, there won't be any scholarships left."

3

COLLEGE IN A SHOPPING BAG

I'D WALKED INTO COACH K'S OFFICE all worried that he was going to pressure me to play point guard, like that was the worst news I could ever hear. Ha. Playing point was nothing compared to this tornado. That not only did I need to *show leadership,* but I also needed to start calling colleges and proving to all the hundreds of coaches out there that I was an all-around versatile, naturally leading player. Which was going to be that much more difficult given that I already had a whole bunch of other strikes against me, like no sophomore season and no summer ball and so-so grades and a family that doesn't have their act together enough to know you have to verbal *two years ahead.*

So now in addition to my gigantic backpack of homework and gigantic duffel of old gym clothes that had been sitting in my gym locker for six weeks getting not so fresh, I had the shopping bag of letters, too, and not a clue in the world where to go. I didn't want to go to the library, that was for sure. It wasn't like I could just sit down and work on Spanish, or think about whatever it was that happened two hundred years ago that I didn't give a hoot about. Not with what was going on inside my head.

I finally ended up parked outside the middle school, wondering if I looked like the moms who were sitting there waiting. Like a middle-aged woman who spent her days driving around Red Bend as an unpaid chauffeur. Had those moms gone to college? Had they had a big old shopping bag of college envelopes once? Was this how I'd end up, when all this was said and done, in twenty or thirty years? Maybe it didn't really matter where I went to college or even if I went at all, not if I was going to end up right back where I'd started, parked outside the Red Bend Middle School gym.

Wow. I'd thought I couldn't feel worse, but would you look at that — now I did.

Curtis showed up finally, and took one look at me and leaned way over against the passenger door. Didn't speak the whole ride home. By the time I noticed, however, it was too late. I mean, if I tried to speak after all that quiet, my first word wouldn't just shatter the silence, it would shatter all the air as well and we'd probably end up suffocating. Which made me feel just that much better, to know I wasn't even connecting with my little brother, who needs all the connections he can get.

But we made it home, finally, and lugged our junk into the warm kitchen, Dad on the phone at the stove while Smut had a little heart attack because I was back and she'd been so worried. At least getting her calmed down helped calm me down a little bit too. And I put the shopping bag in a corner and set the table same as always, listening to Dad say in a tired voice that we were doing just fine.

It's been pretty funny, actually, watching all the Red Bend ladies try to figure out what to do. Normally when there's a big family tragedy — not to sound awful, but it's been a while now with Win, and I guess I'm a little too used to it — well, all the church ladies and town ladies get together and make a bunch of meals they take turns bringing over. Only in our house Dad does the cooking and is totally into it, probably because cooking for him is still new and exciting. And he made it known that we were okay without all that extra food. He'd even given a couple of ladies advice on seasonings, which went over about as well as it would have the other way around, and so now the ladies still wanted to help but hadn't a clue in the world how.

We didn't say too much at supper, though I did ask Curtis how things were going and he said okay, and even admitted he got top score on a science quiz, which you could see made Dad's night, hearing that, and made me pretty happy too, that my brother's so smart and I actually got him to say it out loud. As we were cleaning up Mom called, which she does every night to let us know she's still Mom, and after she caught up with Dad, she said that Win wanted to talk with me.

It should have been nice, the thought of Win getting his special headphones on just to talk to his little sister. But here's the thing: he didn't want to talk *with* me, really; he just wanted to talk *at* me. About practice and all the basketball things I still needed to work on. All I could think about was how much it must suck for Mom to be stuck with him all day long, Win probably on her case nonstop to strengthen her back and lose weight, which on the one hand is a good idea but it wasn't like she didn't have enough going on already. Although it really does make him happy, as happy as he can ever be, to boss folks around, and she'd probably put up with it for that reason alone.

"You really need to start thinking about college, you know." How does he *do* that? He's like a dog that can smell fear, only instead of fear he just sniffs out really awkward conversations.

"Yeah, Win. I've got the letters already."

"What letters?" he asked. If he were a dog, right now his ears would be sticking straight up.

God, I was stupid to bring this up. "Nothing. Just — it's just some mail I got from coaches because of that dumb *People* thing. A whole bunch of them sent letters and stuff."

Win can't move much, but still I could hear him sitting up straighter — sitting up mentally. This was just the sort of thing he'd work to death. "What do they say?"

"I don't know, okay? I just got home. I haven't had time to open them yet."

"Are there any scholarship offers?"

"Yeah, right. No one's going to send me a scholarship like that —"

"You don't know that," Win said sharply. "I know this guy who got written up in *Sports Illustrated,* a tiny article, and he got eleven —"

"Yeah, well, this isn't *Sports Illustrated.*" The only reason that stupid article even got printed was because the *People* people thought it was hilarious that players from rival football teams were going out. It had been one of the reasons Brian and I had broken up, actually, that article. One of the bigger reasons. Which I bet the *People* people wouldn't care about even if they knew. "Listen — I've gotten letters like this before, okay? They'll just say that they're interested in me and I need to get in touch and blah blah blah."

"Because *they* can't call *you,* you know."

"I *know* that." Did Win know he was echoing everything Coach K already told me? "I know they can't call."

"So you need to start calling them. Like tonight."

"I *know!* Will you just — it's been a really long day, okay? My coach is already breathing down my neck about this stuff."

"Because those Division I scholarships don't hang around, you know. I bet some schools have met their quota already. They only have fifteen scholarships total —"

"I know, okay?"

"Men's basketball only has thirteen."

Okay, I didn't know that. That was kind of cool, actually, that women get two more than the men do. That for once women's sports is in the bonus. But I was nowhere near calm enough to absorb that little factoid, let alone discuss it or anything. "Can we please talk about this later?" Like never?

"We need to talk about it now," Win said in his super-annoying reasonable voice. "I mean, this *is* your future."

This time I didn't say *I know.* I thought it. In my brain I was screaming it; if I'd opened my mouth I would probably have broken his eardrum screaming. Instead I just nodded. And sighed this really huge sigh. "Yeah," I said finally. "Listen, I've got homework, okay?"

"Keep me posted on all this."

Like I had a choice. Like Win would ever let it rest. The whole month of November had been one giant Win pressure cooker, him going on and on and on about my training. Which had been good, really it had been, because it meant that I was now in great shape and super ready for the season, and it had also given us something to talk about, and had given Win something to think about beyond the fact he was going to be in a wheelchair for the rest of his life, which is a pretty awful thing to be stuck dwelling on twenty-four hours a day. But that's why it had been so great to get home to Red Bend, because it meant getting away from Win. And now, because I stupidly mentioned those stupid envelopes, I was right back in pressure cooker land.

So, even though I had a ton and a half of homework, I cleared off the kitchen table and dumped the bag of envelopes out. Win was going to call back — maybe even tonight, but definitely in the next few days — and he'd put the screws in me bigtime if I let something as important as this slide (which is how he would phrase it, not even considering the homework I had and the fact that just looking at the envelopes made me feel like crawling under the couch for the entire rest of my life). Then I sat back and stared at the pile.

Curtis wandered in and caught me sitting there looking nine kinds of miserable. I figured he'd back out right away, seeing as misery isn't something he seeks out ever. But instead he took me completely by surprise. "What's this?" he asked, picking an envelope off the floor.

"Basketball," I said, in the tone you'd use to say Projectile Vomiting.

His eyebrows went up. "All these people wrote *you?*"

"Yes, they wrote *me.* Why, is there something wrong with me?"

"No, it's just . . ." He sat down. "You're thinking about San Diego?"

"No, I'm not thinking about San Diego! That's like on the other side of the country."

He looked up at me. "Then why is it here?"

"Because they *mailed* it to me, pea brain —"

"I mean, you should put it in a different pile. A reject pile."

"Oh. Yeah." Since this was only the smartest thing I'd heard all week. And I felt pretty pea-brainish myself for not thinking of it.

We ended up going through the stack, putting most of the envelopes into a cardboard box, and Curtis even wrote TOO FAR AWAY on the outside, just to make the point. He couldn't have been nicer about the whole thing, making jokes about Oklahoma and Arizona and all these other states I can barely find on a map. He even got our beat-up old atlas out of the Caravan so we could see where all these places were, and some of them looked pretty darn far. I mean, as much as I want to be out of Red Bend, I don't want to be out of it forever.

We finally had about a dozen schools in Wisconsin and Minnesota and Michigan's UP, and Iowa and Illinois. And some of them were Big Ten schools, or other state schools like UW–Milwaukee and UM–Duluth. Plus smaller ones I'd never heard of although that doesn't mean much, but at least they were close, close as in a-couple-hours-of-driving close versus taking an airplane. Which is why for example the University of Michigan was right out, because I sure didn't want to have to fly over big old Lake Michigan whenever I wanted to come home.

This was just the first step, I knew, going through those letters. Maybe none of these schools even wanted me anymore, or wouldn't once they got to know me, or maybe they wouldn't have anything left money-wise, and there were probably a million other things I didn't even know to worry about that had already gotten me crossed off their lists. But at least I was doing *something* instead of just sitting around feeling awful, doing something I could report to Win. Plus Curtis started doing this routine, once we got my little pile in order, of going through them and saying "Big Ten! Big Ten!" whenever he got to one of those, with this really goofy grin.

Big Ten — see, Big Ten is a really big deal. Way back when I was a kid, Win explained that it really should be called Big Eleven because there are eleven schools in the conference, but he's right that "Big Eleven" sounds dumb. Big Ten is *really* big when it comes to football — which is why it was such an enormous deal when Bill got that scholarship to the University of Minnesota. It shows what an amazing player he is even if Minnesota doesn't have the world's best team — and it's pretty big in basketball too. Even women's basketball. Not big like Tennessee or Connecticut, but not too far off. So the fact they were sending me letters was pretty darn freaky. Kind of like getting a letter from Santa, or a lottery ticket or something.

That's what they were, really, a pile of lottery tickets. That's what I was looking at.

Then I took an extra-deep breath and started opening

them. I didn't want to, that's for sure, but I knew Win would chew my ear off when he found out I hadn't. And I read them.

Every letter said pretty much the same thing, the first sentence talking about that *People* article and then describing their program, how good it is and their record or their improvement if their record wasn't so good, and how much I would contribute to the team and how I should keep them posted on my season and call them at such and such a number whenever I wanted. The only letter that was a little bit different was from the University of Minnesota, because the U of M coach had a bit more personal stuff to say about how nice my unofficial visit had been and even though I couldn't visit "officially" until next year, I could come by anytime and all I needed to do was call her.

Their sameness was even more obvious the second time I read through them, all of them saying call me, call me, call me right this minute! All those coaches working flat out, even when they're reading *People* magazine if you can believe it, tracking down hoops players, reaching out and reaching out over and over, like fishermen trying to catch fish. And here I was at the other end, a little fish, a tiny little one in little Red Bend, Wisconsin, watching all these hooks go by. And all I could think about was the damage those hooks can do to you, especially if you happen to be a fish.

So when Amber called, I was pretty darn relieved. Because the combination of being told a dozen times *Call me now!* and bloody-fish-hook thoughts and a ton of homework had me ready to run screaming out into the snow.

I snatched up my cell phone. "Hey!"

"Whoa, what's wrong with you?" Amber asked. Because I usually don't sound like a drowning person and she's the rescue boat.

"Nothing. Just school garbage."

"Tell me about it. You know what? They're making me write *all* my English papers. Every single one! Do you know how long *Huckleberry Finn* is? And it's all about guys!"

I couldn't help grinning. "Well, they do make up half the population, you know."

"Yeah, the dumb half . . . So anyway, what are you so bummed about?"

"Nothing." Because I didn't think Amber wanted to hear about my college worries considering her issues just finishing high school. Which I worried about too, don't forget, but all this college business kind of overwhelmed the math quiz stuff. "A math quiz."

"They're making me do all my math homework, too! It's like a million problems. You think they'd cut me a little bit of slack."

"Maybe you could tell them that it's against your religion."

Amber laughed. "Yeah. Statistics is an offense to lesbians. What, you didn't know that?"

"No, I didn't. Tell me more . . ." Listening to Amber while I shoved all the letters back into the shopping bag and shoved the bag and the TOO FAR AWAY box into the office and shut the office door, because I'd done enough for a while.

"Hey," she said, interrupting herself, "what are you doing Friday night? After the game?"

"Nothing." Because I never do anything after games except hang out with Amber. I was glad to hear this wasn't going to change just because she wasn't playing anymore.

"There's this band playing in Prophetstown, Dale says she can get us in. It's supposed to be really awesome —"

All of a sudden I remembered. "Oh. Wait. I think I'm busy."

"Hey, we could just go to the movies or something if you're not into it."

"No, that's not it." I had a feeling this would be awkward. "I just have this thing I promised to go to."

"What?" she asked immediately.

"You know, a thing. Beaner invited me over."

"Beaner Halstaad?" Amber said, like he had fleas or something. Which he doesn't.

"It's just some thing his parents are doing, for the boys' team. I said I'd go."

"The *boys'* team?"

"Yeah. That is what he plays on, you know."

"Are you going to make out with him?"

"No! Jeez, Amber! He's a *friend*, okay?"

"Yeah, right." She sounded more suspicious than Mom. In fact, Mom wouldn't have been suspicious at all, Beaner and I have been buddies so long.

Amber's never been so hot about me having other friends, especially guy friends. Last summer when she caught Brian and me in the middle of a water fight, she pretty much hit the roof. It was like she'd caught us kissing or something. Although now that I think about it, just a few weeks later Brian and I *were* kissing, every chance we got. So maybe that I-wish-we-were-making-out-instead-of-spraying-each-other feeling was in the air when she caught us that day. Maybe Amber has more of a sense of that sort of thing than I ever gave her credit for.

Actually, maybe she does. Because at that moment I considered Beaner as just a friend, and Mom, as suspicious as she gets sometimes, she'd describe him as just a friend without even missing a beat. But of the three of us, guess who turned out to be right?

4
WHOOPSVILLE

IT WAS HARD TO BELIEVE I'd been looking forward to hoops season since September, because now that I was actually practicing, well, let's just say it wasn't so much fun. Coach K was putting the screws in me to *show leadership* every single chance I could, and yelling at me whenever I blew it.

"Jess was open!" he'd yell. "D.J., you saw she was open! Tell Brittany to pass!"

I'd nod and not say a word, because if I was brave enough to talk back to Coach K, I'd be brave enough to tell Brittany to pass to Jess. Of *course* I'd seen that Jess was open — you'd have to be blind not to, which I guess means Brittany is blind because she hadn't seen it on her own. And I was even listening for Kari to tell her; that's how tuned in I was. But by the time I worked up the courage to open my mouth, Brittany passed to a freshman and Kayla intercepted and there went the pinnies' possession.

At least Coach K apologized later, if you could call it apologizing, putting his arm around my shoulder and saying he was sorry for yelling but I really needed to take control. *You need to step up,* he said, over and over, until you'd think there was a staircase right in the middle of the court that I just happened to be missing. And I said I'd try. If I stepped up half as much as I kept saying I'd try to, he'd have stopped yelling.

Tuesday afternoon as we were finishing, Coach K making a big deal of the fact that I'd actually managed to tell a freshman to switch defenders with me, this guy walked up. He'd been in the stands awhile and I figured he was just someone's dad come to watch for a bit.

"So what d'you think?" Coach K asked him, patting me on the back like he hadn't spent the last two hours bawling me out.

"Pretty impressive," the guy said. He shook my hand. "Jerry Knudsen. I coach women at Ibsen College."

"Oh. Hi." Ibsen College . . . Hey! That was in my pile of envelopes. In fact, now that I thought about it, I'd even read that Jerry Knudsen name.

Coach K explained how he and Jerry were friends from way back and Jerry couldn't wait to see me play.

Jerry Knudsen chuckled. "We're just Division III, you know, so we can't offer any athletic scholarships. But I know the folks in admissions. You keep your grades where they are and I'm sure we can offer you a pretty good package, you know, of financial aid."

He knew my grades? I shot Coach K a look.

"I checked your transcript," Coach said. "You'll be fine."
Which was pretty freaky, the thought of him on the computer like that behind my back. Not that I minded, I guess, but still.

"I sure liked what I saw today," Jerry put in.

Coach K patted me again. "Getting this girl to open her mouth . . . But we're coming along."

"You'd be an amazing asset to our team." Jerry looked me over, taking in my height and shoulders, probably even the sweat in my hair. "I'll be here Friday night, that's for sure."

"Oh, yeah. The game."

"You bet. And you should check us out too. We're playing Saturday afternoon." He kept shooting the breeze, filling me in on Ibsen and how their season was going — not too well, although he said it in a lot more roundabout way than that — and repeating that I was basically a shoo-in with admissions. Which was nice to hear.

It was especially nice when Win called that night to bug me *again* on my coach calls and I got to tell him I'd already talked to one.

"Oh yeah? What's the school?"

"Ibsen."

"*Ibsen?* There's no way you're going to a place like that."

"He said my grades were fine!"

"D.J., come on! They're like the bottom of D-III. You'd be totally wasted there."

"Well, he didn't think I'd be wasted."

"Of course he didn't! You're like a dream come true in a place like that! Get real —"

"I *am* real!" Oh, he made me hot! Only Win could twist this great news into something completely terrible. "He came and saw me, you know!"

Win sighed. "You're setting your sights way too low."

At least in the end Win "agreed" — although you'd think I was asking him to give up a kidney or something, the way he went on — that I could wait to call coaches until after I'd seen Ibsen. And I did my best not to slam the phone down when I hung up.

As least school was getting a little easier, the way it always does after a vacation, even a vacation-thingy as long as mine. I was pretty much caught up on homework — I mean, I was still confused, but that was just normal D.J. Schwenk brain confusion; it wasn't like being away had made me smart or anything. Even lunchtimes were okay because I was eating with Beaner. Which meant sitting with all the b-ball guys, and some girls like Kari who can move between different groups without batting a long black eyelash. Beaner had this game he'd made up, sort of table hockey that you played with a fork, defending your tray. It wasn't really my scene, all that joking and yelling, but it would have been way worse sitting alone. Amber wasn't even coming to lunch these days — she was using that time for class work — so really it was Beaner or nothing.

Which makes Beaner sound like a bad choice, which he wasn't, not at all. I guess I was just really aware of how much space his table was taking up, how much cafeteria *atmosphere*. How I would have been watching them if I'd been alone, and how much other kids already were.

Beaner must have sensed how uncomfortable I was sometimes, because he'd sit next to me and joke around, doing play-by-play on the table hockey.

"So, Miss Schwenk," he'd murmur, using a hot dog bun for a microphone, "I understand you were present at last year's finals when Tyler choked — and look folks, he did it again! Right in the Jell-O! And isn't that gross — he's actually licking it off! Dude! Is it true that his jeans fell down at that event? Describe to the audience just what he was wearing under his jeans. That is, if he was wearing *anything*. There have been rumors, you know."

He didn't really expect me to answer; he just got a kick out of making me laugh.

Plus, a couple days I had lunch, or *almuerzo* I should say, with Mrs. LeVoir, to work on Spanish. Which was a completely different experience, you can be sure.

And then came Friday night's game.

We won, don't get me wrong. We were playing Coopesville, which everyone calls Whoopsville, so if we'd lost it would have been a total disaster. And I scored a bunch of points, but I played really badly. Coach K was pushing me *so* hard on the leadership thing, and getting so mad at me when I flubbed it. But no matter how bad it got, he wouldn't sub me out, even when I finally just panicked and started driving in for lay-ups even though I was double-teamed because that was easier than telling four other girls what to do.

And it didn't help, believe me, that Jerry Knudsen was sitting right behind our bench. I could even see the two of them talking, which I'm sure isn't allowed in the gazillion pages of NCAA recruiting rules, although maybe with bottom-of-the-barrel D-III they aren't so picky. Anyway, whenever I looked over, Coach K and Jerry Knudsen were jawing it up.

But here's the weird thing: after the game was over and we were gathering up our stuff, Jerry Knudsen came over with a big smile to tell me how fantastic I'd been.

I shot Coach K an eyeball like, *See?* And Coach agreed that I'd had a couple great plays even if I couldn't even speak — which he didn't say but it was implied.

"You'd be some kind of special for Ibsen, I'll tell you that," Jerry said. "And don't worry about us being too small —"

"I wasn't," I said really fast. Because it hadn't occurred to me for one thing, and even if it had, it was still *college.*

"You folks played Madison a few years back, dintcha?" Coach K asked.

"Oh yeah. Got a new gym floor out of it too. Seeing as it was a money game and all," he explained to me.

"Wow, Madison. How'd you do?" Because *money game* means a big powerful school pays a little weak one to play them, and the big school almost always wins by a lot. It's really awful sometimes, how badly the little school gets beat.

"Oh, you don't focus on that, you just take your payment and say thanks . . . So, you coming tomorrow?"

"I'll try. I need to see that new floor." If he wasn't going to make a big deal out of losing so badly, then neither was I. Besides, it must have been worth it, because gym floors are really expensive.

He laughed. "That's the spirit now. I'll keep an eye out for you. Just tell them at the front desk who you are."

"Do I need a pass or anything, or tickets?"

He laughed again, and shook my hand and left. Which I took to mean that I didn't. Then I went and showered and tried to think about something very different from Ibsen, which was Beaner Halstaad's party.

I've always liked Beaner — I mean, everyone likes him, he's that kind of guy. But we've always had a special kidding-around thing, like the way he jumps on my back. Even after he used that *date* word, though, I didn't think about him as anything but a friend. And then I got to the party and found a bunch of guys out back grilling brats even though it was twenty degrees outside, because that's Wisconsin, you can't keep us from our sausages. They were also sneaking sips from a bottle someone brought, because I guess that's a Wisconsin thing too.

I didn't have much interest in freezing my feet off watching brats grill and guys drink, so I hung around in the living room with some other guys and their parents until Beaner's little sister Abby and her buddy Gabby dragged me away. Abby's actually Beaner's half sister, nine years old and just as skinny and bouncy as he is, and she and Gabby took me up to her bedroom and sat me down in a corner and started playing with my hair even though it's only five inches long, and basically treated me like I was some kind of princess if princesses are six feet tall and all spent from a hoops game.

At one point they started giggling extra crazy, and whispering like they had the world's biggest secret, and finally Abby put her arms around my neck and whispered in my ear with her hot tickly breath, "Beaner likes you!" Then they collapsed on each other.

I blushed, although the room was pretty dark, thank God. "Yeah, he's a good friend."

"He's not a *friend*," Abby said. "He's your *boyfriend*."

"No, he's not. Did, um, did he tell you this?"

Which made the two girls almost die, they were giggling so hard. "No!" Abby said. "He just asked me what he should wear tonight" (I guess it's never to early to start going to girls — some girls, anyway — for fashion advice) "and he showed me your picture and asked what I thought."

Here's what's scary: this kid was only nine and already she knew more about guys and dating than I did. "So what'd you say?"

"I said . . ." Abby frowned. "I said you were a real girl, not like some girls" (see what I mean about scary? Also, what does that even mean?) "and he needed to be really nice to you."

"And *kiss* you," Gabby broke in. Which sent them right back into giggle land.

And of course right at that moment Beaner popped in looking for me, which sent all *three* of us into giggles. I couldn't help it — I mean, I'm not a giggler normally, but you can understand.

"Whassup?" he asked, looking at us like we were crazy, which he had every right to do.

"Nothing," I managed to say, which sent us off again. And then when Beaner pulled me up — actually touching my hand! — the girls almost passed out.

"Your sister's really cute," I said as we walked off, trying to ignore the racket behind us.

"She's a total pain in the butt." Beaner grinned, and shot me a look like maybe he knew what we'd been talking about, but right away I asked about his game to change the subject. Although I guess the subject didn't get changed all that much because we ended up in *his* bedroom somehow, and there was this little pause, and he leaned toward me and I leaned toward him . . .

Grandpa Warren — Dad's dad, who Win was named after — he had some pretty strange tastes in food. It's a wonder we like anything normal considering how much he loved pigs' feet and blood sausage and head cheese, all these strange meats that you eat when it's your own animals and you can't waste one little bit. And even though by the time I was born we weren't slaughtering anymore, Grandpa Warren still liked that sort of stuff, yuck, and a couple times a year Mom would buy him a beef tongue. Seriously. Because he liked them so much. She'd go to a special butcher because it's not like the Super Saver carries them, and bring home this huge gray *tongue* all wrapped in paper, and spend a couple days slicing it up on bread with lots of mustard while Grandpa Warren told her how great it was and us kids stood around trying not to barf. Well, the older kids did. Curtis was probably into it, he's such a freak.

Anyway, I hadn't thought about Grandpa Warren's tongue sandwiches in years, but I couldn't help it while I was making out with Beaner. Brian — why did he keep coming up all the time? I wasn't supposed to think about him anymore, ever! He was like a cut you think is healed but it just keeps reopening. I hated — *hated* — comparing him to Beaner. But it was so hard not to. Because even though Brian was the only other guy I'd kissed, I'd known right from the beginning that he was pretty good. Not that I'm going to go into detail, thank you, but he wasn't pushy, unless it was so hot and heavy that you had to be pushy, if you know what I mean. But I guess Beaner had a whole different philosophy. It was okay, don't get me wrong, but I didn't feel *on fire* like I had with Brian. I mean, I like Beaner, but still. So after a while I asked if we could go back downstairs to get a couple of pops, because that seemed fun too.

And then as I was leaving the party, he walked me out and we kissed again beside the Caravan.

"So," I asked during a breath, "why are we doing this?"

"You're not familiar with this ritual? The whole lip-locking thing?"

"That's not what I meant! Why — why, you know, me?"

Beaner laughed out loud. "You really don't know?"

"Uh, no . . ." Had someone had set him up? Daring him to make out with big dumb D.J.?

"Come on! All those times we hung out together after football games — getting lunch during preseason — why do you think I was there?"

"Um . . ." I said, wishing I had five hours to remember all the conversations we'd had at Taco Bell. On the field. Had I really not even noticed Beaner was into me?

"Because of you," he put in.

"Great."

"No, really." Beaner pulled me a little closer, and I have to say it felt awfully nice, the way our bodies fit together. Like two puzzle pieces. "Anyway, I was thinking how maybe now that you were free, you know, maybe this could work. Between us. If, you know, you wanted it to."

"Wow," I said, extremely intelligently. "Wow."

"Yeah. Wow." He gave me another kiss. Which would have lasted who knows how long, but luckily my phone started ringing, and I quick wiped off my mouth and grabbed it: Mom.

"Um, I gotta get this."

"That's cool." He shot me a grin — a boyfriend grin. "So . . . see you around."

I have to admit my stomach did a little flip, seeing that. Boyfriend grins are pretty special. But I was also trying to start the Caravan and answer the phone and wave goodbye, so my stomach was competing with a lot of other muscles. Plus Mom kept going on about how it was too late to call and I had to keep saying it wasn't, which when you think about it doesn't make any sense, that I should be apologizing to the person who called me. I didn't tell her I'd just left a party because she'd totally freak about me *talking on a cell phone* while *driving in the dark* after *possibly drinking* with *other teenagers*. Better that I didn't have any friends and spent all my time alone in a cave. Which is what our house is basically, so she shouldn't worry.

"Is everything all right?" I asked finally, even though I wasn't really listening to her because I was so busy thinking about

Beaner. He'd said I was free. *Free* as in *available.* That meant he'd been paying attention to me and Brian.

"Oh, everything's fine. Win's asleep now, you know, so we can talk a bit, just us two."

"Oh. Okay." How did Beaner know about Brian? Besides *People,* I mean? Although now that I thought about it, Beaner had talked about him even during preseason. He knew somehow even back then that Brian worked for us! Was he thinking about me way back in August? And I hadn't even noticed?

"Win would never tell you himself — you know how he is — but we're both so grateful for all this college business. You know, you're getting him the very best possible therapy."

Wait — that got my attention. "What? I'm getting Win *therapy?*"

"Oh, yeah. You should have seen him this afternoon on the computer. I'm not sure he'd even be making the effort, getting a special keyboard and all, if it wasn't for you. Going to websites, looking at schools . . . He knows more about Ibsen College now than Ibsen does, probably!"

"Super."

"Oh, D.J., it is." She took a deep breath, like she was steeling herself. "You know, don't you, how important all this is? You don't want to spend the rest of your life milking cows. You *need* college, you know — it's your ticket off the farm. Well, I've got to go now, honey, but you . . . Don't forget that now, will you? Don't forget."

⑨ ⑨ ⑨ ⑨

You don't want to spend the rest of your life milking cows. Did I not know this? Of course I needed college to get out of Red Bend! I remembered it every second of the day! But I'd never realized Mom knew it too. I'd never heard her say it, say so bluntly, that I needed to *escape.* She sounded desperate . . .

You know what this meant? If I didn't make it — didn't get into college — I'd be totally disappointing her.

Not to mention Win. Who apparently was taking on all this occupational therapy work just for me. Which I did not ask for, thank you very much, but was now feeling ten thousand pounds of guilt about. If I didn't get in, he'd spend the rest of his life reminding me that I blew it. Maybe not with words necessarily, but he'd be thinking it. Every time we were together, he'd think it, every family reunion for the rest of my life. Mom would be disappointed, but with Win it'd be flat-out disgust.

Win would be flat-out disgusted with tonight's game, that's for sure. We'd beaten Whoopsville, yeah, but only because the rest of the team stood around while I hogged all the baskets. Whatever leadership is, I'd demonstrated just the opposite. Coach K worked and worked but I couldn't manage a single squeak, no matter how hard he tried. That college coach had said nice things about me, sure, but only because Coach K was his friend. I'd let K down, and that coach, and all the girls on the team, girls who never got a chance to play because I couldn't even manage to pass the ball. "Asset to the team" — ha. Tonight I'd been the worst kind of athlete possible.

You know who else I'd let down, let down already? Beaner. I hadn't even known he was interested in me! For months, maybe, and I hadn't noticed. What does that say about me, huh? About my abilities with guys? I don't even know what dating is. It took a nine-year-old to explain that I was even *on* one. Talk about clueless.

Thinking all these thoughts, these horrible true thoughts . . . by the time I got home, I was almost puking, I was so upset. Remember way back on Monday when I was so freaked out by all that locker-decorating, we-have-a-date, D.J.-is-#1 attention? Well, guess what: my panic had turned out to be totally legitimate. All these people, Beaner and Coach K and the team and college scouts, and Mom and Win most of all, they all were focused on *me,* and expecting things from me — leadership and college scholarships and girlfriendness.

Well, leadership I'd already failed at. Scholarships I was about to. And romance . . . the record was pretty clear on that one already. With romance, I was zero for life.

I already knew I was a loser. Someone who didn't measure up, not when the pressure was on. Now it was just a matter of everyone else figuring it out too.

Oh, wouldn't that be fun.

5
SNAKE-FILLED ENVELOPES

WELL, IF YOU THOUGHT I got hit by a disaster on Friday night, check out the weekend. Because Saturday I drove to Ibsen College. With *Dad* of all people, who actually drove two whole hours away from his cows after I promised we'd be back for evening milking. I'd been planning on going by myself, but at breakfast he volunteered to come along. Maybe Mom had put the screws in him, who knows — it's certainly not the sort of thing he does normally. As soon as he spoke up, I started thinking up all the ways he could embarrass me, bragging about his cows or asking if anyone knew about organic farming or scratching himself in a weird way; with Dad the list is pretty much endless. But there wasn't much I could do but say yes. And bite my tongue not to warn him to behave, because that'd just make him worse.

At least he let me drive, which was nice of him, although Dad's a big fan of napping in cars, and if you got up at five a.m. every day you probably would be too. So after we chatted about milk prices and his new organic co-op Internet buddies, and Bill's chances of going pro, which if nothing else reminded me that I wasn't the only one dealing with long-shot lottery tickets, Dad put his seat back and dozed off while I thought some more about college.

I wasn't completely uninformed on the subject, I hope you know. I'd visited the University of Minnesota, after all, and seen Tyrona's dorm room — she's on the hoops team and super cool — and even eaten in the team cafeteria, which was pretty wild, seeing all that food and knowing athletes could have whatever they wanted. And I'd spent a bunch of hours walking around and looking at the U of M students and the buildings too, pretending I was one of them — the students, I mean, not the buildings — and being very into the whole college experience. Although maybe it was different at Ibsen. But I hoped not.

Here's the thing: Ibsen is very different from the U of M, in every possible way.

First of all, it's tiny in comparison to the University of Minnesota, which has a huge hospital and buildings with tubes coming out of them and fifty thousand students. Ibsen has less than a thousand students, and their whole campus could fit in one block of the U of M, probably. And their gym — well, their gym is about the size of Red Bend High School's. Even with the new floor.

We didn't have any trouble parking — Dad said students were probably gone for the weekend. And the gym just had a student sitting at the entrance who didn't even let Dad finish his sentence before waving us through. So you can see how tight security was.

And then when we got to the basketball court there was hardly anyone there. Red Bend's JV games get about three times the turnout. Maybe it was just because it was a girls' game — I mean a *women's* game, which is so hard for me to remember to say it like that — or everyone goes home on Saturday, or maybe the team wasn't having much of a season. But we found seats right near the center line without any trouble at all.

And then the two teams came out and, well, some of the players looked a lot like Ashley Erdel, on both teams, and none of the players looked like me. They didn't play like me, either. I hate to sound so stuck up, but it's the truth, I won't lie. Jerry Knudsen was right there in the thick of it of course, being the coach, though he waved to us and kept looking back to check on me. Gave me a thumbs-up when one of his players landed a three-pointer.

So we watched the game, which was about like a Red Bend game — well, like a Red Bend game if I wasn't playing. Again, to be honest. And if Kari wasn't playing either. Dad didn't say too much except for cheering the good shots, the good Ibsen shots. The score was pretty close, actually, and Ibsen was within four at halftime. Then the teams went into their locker rooms and some girls — women — came out to do this dance routine with a pep band that only had about four musicians, and Dad settled back a little and looked around the gym.

"Not much of a crowd, is it?"

"Nope," I said.

"I went to a Badgers" — meaning the University of Wisconsin–Madison — "game once. I'd never seen that many people before all in one place." He laughed to himself. "I thought for a minute the roof was going to fall in, we were making so much noise. That was a night, all right." He glanced over at me. "You could play like that, you know."

"You mean worrying about the roof?" But I grinned when I said it.

"This isn't your league, sport. You come here and you'd be the whole team."

He had a point. This was awfully small potatoes compared to Big Ten basketball. Granted, that had been a men's game Dad went to; he'd never watch a women's game if he didn't have a daughter. But you know, the University of Minnesota arena *sells out* for women's games — that's how much folks in Minneapolis care about women's hoops. It sells out almost as much for women as it does for men. Which is pretty awesome to think about.

The second half started and Ibsen started losing, bit by bit, and Dad started getting fidgety about his cows, and so the next time Jerry Knudsen looked back I waved to him and gestured that we were leaving. We wandered around the campus for a few more minutes, checking out the other buildings, pretty old brick ones and modern concrete ones that looked awfully cold, the main building with an IBSEN COLLEGE sign and some lumpy snow-covered shrubs. Then we hit the road.

Now I could really see what Jerry Knudsen meant about turning their program around — it'd be pretty much a 180 with me there. I'd get plenty of playing time, that's for sure. And the classes wouldn't be too hard, either. I'm sure you're wondering how I could tell that just from looking at the buildings, but I could. Which is something to think about as well, particularly considering that the whole point of college is to get educated in something beyond three-pointers. It'd be nice to do that without getting ulcers in the process.

"Whatcha thinking?" Dad asked.

I shrugged. "Ibsen is small. But that's not a bad thing."

"You're bigger than that place, sport."

"The coach said he could get me money."

"Of course he'd say that. They'd win their conference with you playing, sure as shooting."

"And winning's bad?"

He looked out his window. "I'd sure like to see you playing in a real arena."

Which meant that now I was going to disappoint him too. We got back way before milking, not that I was sweating that one, and right away Mom called. She wanted to hear all about Ibsen, and sounded so pleased that Dad had gone with me — he'd get lots of points for that — and was her usual positive self, saying how nice it was that there might be financial aid for me.

Then Win got on and asked what the players had been like.

"They were okay," I said.

"Huh. I checked them out online — you know what their record is?"

"I'd get lots of playing time —" I started, but then Dad took the phone right out of my hand.

"Hey there, son . . . Well, yeah, of course I told her. You know what she's like." What did that mean, *what I was like?* "Uh-huh . . . Oh, I told her . . . You betcha." Dad handed me the phone.

I picked it up like it was covered in cow poop. "What?"

"Are you going to make those calls now?"

"They offered me money. Remember you said I'd get offered something? Well, Ibsen did. The coach said he could get me a pretty good package. Those were like his exact words."

"You're wimping out, kiddo. First of all, until you have something in writing, don't believe anything a coach promises. And you can't look at just one college —"

I snorted. I couldn't help it. Is it clear that I didn't want to make those calls? That I'd rather clean the barn bare-handed? And knowing Win was right didn't make it any easier.

"Jeez, D.J., what is wrong with you?"

I really wanted to say *What's wrong with YOU?* But even I had the brains to know how mean that would be. Plus thanks to Mom I now knew that my college recruiting had somehow become part of Win's recovery, which is just the sort of thing that Win can do, take something that's someone else's business and completely make it his. So I couldn't just hang up on him, no matter how much I wanted to, because that would be interfering with his *therapy.* "I don't want to call those people," I said finally.

"Well, duh. But no one else can do it for you. You want Dad doing it? What are you, ten?"

I gritted my teeth, trying to be nice for Mom's sake. Trying. "No, I don't want Dad —"

"You want me to call first? Let them know you'll be contacting them?"

Silence.

Win sighed. "You want me to call?"

"You're so much better at it . . ." Now trying to be super nice because it was an extremely good suggestion.

"D.J., I can't even dial."

I didn't have the guts to say that dialing a phone — or however SCI patients do it, with big push buttons I'm guessing — that that would be really good therapy. Although even Win's saying that aloud is impressive, to actually admit he had a weakness, which he's never been so good at before . . .

Then the old bossy Win kicked in again. "This is your responsibility, kid. Start with U of M. The coach already knows you. You need to call her *now*. You need to call her tonight —"

Finally I couldn't take any more, no matter how therapeutic it might be for Win to boss me around. "Can I talk to Mom again?"

"Mom?"

"You know, our mother? Can I talk to her?"

So Win sighed, and there was this noise as they switched from his headset to a real phone, all the while Win grumbling. Nothing I could make out, but he definitely wasn't pleased.

Only Mom was double-teaming me with him. "So honey, you going to make those calls?"

"It's Saturday night, Mom —"

"Well, I'm sure you can leave a message, you know. I'm sure they're all set up for that. You really need to get on this."

I got off the phone finally, and then Dad of all people handed me the big grocery bag of recruiting letters. Now I was getting *triple*-teamed. I sat there staring at the envelopes, too scared to even touch them. Which is stupid, I know, because how dangerous can an envelope be? It's not like there are snakes or something inside. Or rats, yuck. But you'd have thought there were cobras tucked into those letters, the way I was looking at them.

Curtis caught on pretty quick what I was up to because he started tiptoeing around like someone had died — he gets the dry heaves around a phone normally, let alone a high-stakes situation like this. And Dad patted me on the shoulder with a "Good luck, sport." Finally I took the phone and envelopes and went into the little office off the kitchen, Smut curled up beside me with her tail thumping at how exciting this all was, and all my letters that might be my ticket to college. And I didn't throw up. But I got pretty close once or twice.

All the coaches, all the letters, said I could call whenever, which was crazy because what if I called at two a.m.? Although I guess it'd be pretty stupid of a prospect to demonstrate she can't even tell time. Maybe it was too late already . . . Although it wasn't late at all. It wasn't even suppertime yet.

If I didn't get this done, Win would eat me alive. And then Mom would come over to my dead, eaten body and say how disappointed she was that I wasn't helping Win's therapy. And then Coach K and everyone else in school would say how unsurprised they were that it had taken me so little time to screw up, that of course I'd fail at phone calls considering I couldn't even manage point guard . . . It was like every person I knew was squeezed into that little office with me, whispering what a loser I was.

Smut licked my hand and gave me one of those worried looks she's so good at, like no matter what anyone said she still loved me. Which was a boost. And it got me to pick up the phone and dial, hoping like crazy it'd go to voice mail, although what would I say *then*? I hadn't even thought about that, which is so stupid because that's one thing that's actually easy and doable. I should have at least written something down . . .

Here's what I can remember of the U of M call:

A WOMAN: Hello?

ME: Um, hello. This is D.J., um, Schwenk. I met you like a month ago —

HER: Oh, yes, D.J.! (How could she remember me like that? She has hundreds of girls to keep track of.) It's great to hear from you.

ME: Oh . . .

HER: So how are you doing?

ME: Um, okay . . . Is this a good time? You know, to call?

HER: Sure it is. You sound a little nervous.

ME: Well, yeah. A little . . .

HER: Well, you shouldn't be. This is just a chance for the two of us to get to know each other a bit. No pressure at all.

ME: Oh. We had our first game yesterday —

HER: You know, we can talk basketball later. Right now I'm a lot more interested in you. You know, I didn't have a chance to ask earlier — do you have any pets?

ME: Yeah. A dog. (Smut immediately tries to climb into my lap.)

HER: What's his name — or her name? Is it a boy or a girl?

ME: Her name is Smut . . . It's goofy, I know.

HER: (Laughing.) It's a great name. I bet there's a great story behind it.

ME: Not really . . .

By this time I was sweating so bad, the phone was practically sliding out of my hand. I don't know why I was sweating, because as you can see the coach couldn't have been nicer. But just knowing I had to talk was a killer.

Eventually, though, my heart stopped pounding quite so much, and I figured out how to hold the phone with a tissue to soak up the sweat, and I actually, you know, communicated. She asked how Win was doing, and was super nice to ask if I even wanted to talk about him and his accident and stuff. You'd think I wouldn't considering how many hours I'd talked about it already, but sometimes there's still stuff to say. So instead of saying he was okay, I described what recovery means when you've got a C5-C6 incomplete stable spinal cord injury. Although I left out the part about how he's a total pain in the butt. And she said she'd love to have me visit again soon, and that the U of M was having a great season so far and she'd like to see me play and maybe if she was in Wisconsin sometime she would.

I didn't get bitten by snakes, not once. But when I got off the phone I was shaking, I was so spent. It was just talking, I know, but it was the hardest talking I'd ever done. Plus she hadn't even wanted to talk sports, which is the one topic I'm halfway decent at! My voice was all scratchy too. All I wanted to do . . .

All I wanted to do was to talk to Brian Nelson. There. I'll admit it. After all that torture, I wanted to talk to the only person I've ever been able to really *talk* to. Like over the summer when we were painting the barn. Or this fall when I was stuck in Seattle with Win, and Win was refusing to talk to the doctors or anyone else or to me. During that time Brian and I talked every day, for hours sometimes. And sure, we'd gab about Brian's football season and movies and funny things that had happened, but he also helped me understand what was going on with Win, to get inside Win's head better than anyone else in the world could, and whenever I complained he'd just agree that it sounded really hard without ever once saying I was wimping out, or criticizing Win either, which would have been just as tough to hear. I've never in my life known anyone as good at talking as Brian, talking in a understanding, heart-to-heart way without all that baggage and pretending that most people clog up their conversations with.

Right now I missed Brian more than I had in weeks. Missed him as much as I had right after we'd broken up. Well, *right* after we broke up I was too angry to do much missing, too mad that this guy who was so fantastic at talking turned out to be such a jerk in public, especially when that public included his friends. But after I got over being angry at him, I was just sad. Especially when I was really low, when I really needed someone to lean on. Right now, if the two of us were talking, Brian would agree that calling coaches was really hard, and he'd get me to laugh, and boost me up enough to continue with the other coaches on my list.

I couldn't call Brian, though, for a bunch of reasons that should be very extremely obvious.

There were other people in my life, however. There was even a guy in my life, thank you very much, a guy who's always totally upbeat, and who *kissed* me. Which, duh, would make him the absolute best person to talk to now, because a boyfriend is someone who's good for more than just making out, right? A boyfriend is someone who's there for you.

Beaner was home — although I called his cell, so I guess that doesn't matter too much, does it? — and right away, before I even had time to explain about calling coaches and how I wasn't having the most fun in the history of the world, he asked what I wanted my ring tone to be.

I don't think much about ring tones except when they're annoying. "Anything that's not annoying."

He laughed. "How about 'A Little Less Conversation'?"

"Oh. Um, how can you talk without conversation?"

"You're hilarious! No, Elvis, you spaz! The King! You know, his song?"

"Oh. You mean that's the title of a song?"

"Come on, you know it, you've got to. Here, I'll play it for you . . ."

It was a cool song, I admit, even though I'd never pick it out for me. Besides, I wasn't interested in ring tones — I wanted to talk. But I didn't have the energy, the talking skills, to explain that to Beaner. Especially at that moment. So I just thanked him for the ring tone idea and promised he could set up my phone too, if he wanted, and said goodbye.

And then really fast I called three other coaches, leaving messages for them because thank *God* they weren't available, or maybe they were but they didn't want to hear from SCHWENK, WARREN, which is our caller ID left over from Grandpa Warren because we've never changed the phone bill. And then on the next day — on *Sunday,* if you can believe it — Coach K called me to say that I needed to call those people back, because apparently even if you leave a message for a coach they can't call you, they can only call your coach or principal or stuff. Which they'd just done to Coach K to make sure he'd prod me to call them again. So I did, going back into our little office with the phone and Smut and my box of tissues, and each one of them said how much they wanted me to visit their schools, and we talked about basically the same stuff I had with the U of M lady, and by the end of the third conversation my pulse was pretty close to normal because I was getting so used to it all.

So I guess you could say that the weekend ended a lot better than it began, although that wasn't so hard, because when you're at the bottom all directions point up.

6
A Short Little Genius B-Ball Player

Monday in school, though, i was bummed again. Everyone kept talking about our big victory over Coopesville, no one saying that if we — if I — played like that against a real team we'd get creamed. And then even Ibsen wouldn't be interested in me.

I sat there in health class wishing we were shooting baskets instead of studying nutrition. Shooting baskets at least is good for you instead of sitting at a stupid desk feeling your butt grow.

Speaking of folks who could benefit from some b-ball drills, Ashley Erdel was taking health class even though she's a senior. Because you have to take it to graduate and she missed it last year because she took physics instead, and don't even get me started on why someone who volunteers for physics has to take a class as dumb as health. She looked totally bummed too, not even paying attention to the teacher. Well, no one was, but Ashley usually faked it at least.

When someone on your team is bummed, it's your responsibility to help. I slipped over beside her. "What's wrong?" I whispered.

She groaned. "SATs. I just got my scores."

Just hearing the word *SAT* — well, the letters — made my stomach clench up. Because guess how good I'll be at *those*. "Oh. I'm sure you did okay . . ."

"I'll never get in." She stabbed her pen at the UW–Madison logo on the cover of her notebook that went with the UW–Madison sweatshirt she was wearing.

"You're like the smartest kid in school!"

She shot me this look. "Do you have any idea how competitive it is? It's not just grades — it's scores and how 'rounded' you are. Why do you think I'm playing basketball?"

Oh. That explained it. She was playing because of college. Just like me in a way if you think about it, although I also happened to actually like basketball. And be good at it. "Well, that's good, then, because basketballs are round. You know, to help you get rounded?"

That got her smiling at least. Which was nice, that I could cheer her up.

It didn't do my mood any good, though. Because you know what this meant? If even Ashley Erdel, with her A+ grades and the physics classes she takes for fun, if she was freaked about getting into college, what did that say about the prospects for me?

☉ ☉ ☉ ☉

I chewed on that all day, how much the whole college application process sucked even for super-smart kids who should just be getting into Madison automatically. Plus Ashley was completely lost at practice. It was — well, it was exactly what would happen if I decided to take physics to round out *my* application. I'd be sweating just as much as she was, and she was sweating a lot. We were playing three on three on three, which is a great way to practice defense, but she had no idea what she was doing, and this freshman she was guarding kept stepping around her and getting the pass. Every time. Poor Ashley was almost in tears.

We were walking back to the locker rooms afterward and Ashley said — to me, but she could have said it to anyone; I just happened to be next to her at the time — "I stink."

Which was true, but you can't agree. I tried to think of some way to point out that if this were physics class *I* would stink, but I was smart enough at least to know that my words would get all jumbled on the way out and just make things worse. So I said the one thing I thought probably wouldn't hurt too much: "I could help if you wanted."

She looked up. "Really?"

"There are some tricks to guarding, if you're interested."

So to make a long story short, the two of us ended up in the cafeteria. Which used to be the girls' gym back in the days when folks didn't think girls were good enough for the real gym. Coach K even got us permission.

There were still lines on the floor from when girls practiced here, and where little kids still do on Saturday mornings, which was good news for me, because that's what I needed most, the lines. Because even though Ashley couldn't shoot, she could guard at least. I hoped. So we ran through a bunch of things, how to position yourself, how to watch your man's feet and her eyes, how to keep your knees bent and your hands up. Ashley kept fouling me, every couple of seconds, it seemed, and every time she did I'd make her shoot five free throws, because that's such good practice and also because she needed to learn not to foul!

Actually, it was a lot like what I did with Brian Nelson last summer, this training stuff, except easier even because I wasn't thinking every second how cute Ashley was and how nice she smelled, which had always been sort of a distraction with Brian, those thoughts. Plus she didn't complain. Brian might be fantastic at talking, but at workouts he'd gripe like it was prison camp or something. Not Ashley, though. She'd just try again, even though it was obviously so difficult for her, figuring out where to put her feet and how to get her arms to work. It was like her body didn't belong to her, you know what I mean? Like if she focused on one part, another part would just go off and do whatever it felt like and then she'd foul me again. If nothing else, it was a really good lesson in how being a Schwenk actually has some advantages.

I kept telling her to box me out and she'd say, "Okay," and then I'd get right past her. And then she'd have to do ten sit-ups, but I'd do them too to keep her company. And then I'd get past her again. After a while it occurred to me that maybe she didn't know what I was talking about. Like if it was me taking physics I'd be nodding but inside I'd be thinking, *Whatever.* "You know what 'box out' means?"

Ashley nodded, kind of.

"Okay," I said, straightening for a minute. "You know — you know in math sometimes there are those problems with an x? And sometimes there's both the x thingy and the y?"

"Sure. Multivariable equations."

Sheesh, I thought, but I didn't say it aloud. "Yeah. Them. Well, you're defending, right? And you don't want your man — *me* — you don't want me to get the ball. You want to keep me out of play. And a pass could come from either direction. It could come from over there, which is x" — I waved in her direction — "or it could come from here, behind me. That's y, behind me. Right?"

Ashley nodded slowly.

"Right. Well, if you push me right up against the line, who's over there in y to pass to me?"

"Um, nobody? Because it's out of bounds?"

"Exactly! So your job as a defender is to take that, um, multa . . ."

"Multivariable equation —"

"Yeah, and turn it into just an *x*. Which is you. Can you think of it that way?"

Ashley nodded, not so slowly this time, and we started again. And guess what? She got it! She was still fouling like crazy, but at least she'd figured out how important it was not to let me get around her. Which was pretty great.

Plus we worked on her foul shooting, where to aim, and how to hold the ball. I'd learned from working with Brian that it's important not to dump a whole bunch of information on someone all at once, not to be like, *You're bad at this and this and this and this,* because who wants to hear that? Instead we just focused for a while on her feet, and then her stance, and then her aim, me trying each time to be just as nice as I'd been with Brian, trying to be all trainer-ish like I'd been this summer.

"What are you thinking?" I asked once as she was standing there dribbling at the line — and looking a heck of a lot better than she had forty-five minutes earlier if I do say so myself.

"About my feet?" she answered, like it was a test.

"Well, yeah. Because that's important. But a lot of players also think a little thing each time they're at the line, sort of a little chant or something so they can focus."

"Like a mantra," Ashley said.

"Uh . . . sure." I grabbed a ball and demonstrated, dribbling hard six times as I whispered to myself, getting my head into the game.

"What are you saying?"

I grinned. "I can't tell you that. That's like asking what you wish for when you blow out your birthday cake."

"But it helps?"

"It's *essential*," I said, feeling totally trainer-ish.

Well, maybe she made up something and maybe she didn't, but her free throwing did get better. Meaning it was looking better even if the ball didn't go in. And she was a *lot* better at defending — again, any direction is up when you're on the bottom — and even a bit more aggressive. Which was something else she needed to work on.

I felt bad that I'd kept her from homework, but she didn't look like she minded too much. It was only one day, after all. You can really improve in one day if you set yourself to it, and she was. Finally we stopped, totally pooped, Ashley for obvious reasons, and me from having to be so supportive and also from trying my darnedest not to knock her down when she was guarding me. Sometimes playing *non*aggressively is just as hard as the other way around.

"I feel like I know you a lot better now," Ashley said kind of shyly as we were gathering up our sweatshirts and balls.

"Isn't that funny? I was thinking the same thing." I laughed. "I feel like my brain is twice as big, just from hanging out around you."

"Me too," Ashley said, laughing herself. Which was nice even if it wasn't true.

Only how smart were we? Because the custodians had locked all the doors and we couldn't get back to the gym. Which meant we had to go outside in just our shorts and bang on the gym door so the guys would let us in. Beaner was the one who did, and he grinned like it was the funniest thing ever to see us standing out there shivering.

"Well, hello there, ladies. What's the magic word?"

"*Please,*" said Ashley, rolling her eyes.

Beaner grinned even wider as he opened the door, but he was grinning at me. His boyfriend grin. My stomach did a flip, seeing it. It's awfully nice having a guy smile at you like that.

"Wanna play a little one-on-one?" he asked, bouncing me his ball.

"Beaner!" his coach called. "Practice?"

"In a sec," Beaner said, but he didn't stop grinning. "Shoot from here. I dare you."

A couple guys heard him and stopped what they were doing to watch. Ashley did too.

I was past the midcourt line. It would be one heck of a basket if I made it.

I bounced a couple times, whispering my free-throw chant, and powered a shot. I really thought I had it — the ball even circled the rim — but at the last second it dropped away.

Everyone groaned, which was nice, and Beaner did this little victory dance about how I almost made it, until their coach blew his whistle and Ashley and I went into the locker room.

"So, do you want to do it again?" she asked as we started changing.

I laughed. "I really don't think it's worth practicing shots like that . . ."

"No, not that . . . I was just thinking — you're probably way too busy, never mind — I was just thinking that maybe we could, you know . . ." She glanced over, too shy to look at me directly. "That we could maybe make this coaching a regular thing."

Well, that was something to think about, all right. How to turn Ashley Erdel into something other than a very intelligent benchwarmer. Or rather, how to *try* to turn her, because all the things that Ashley was so intelligent about couldn't be applied to basketball. And even if they could, it wasn't like I could make every situation into some fancy math equation just so she'd be able to understand what I was talking about.

But I had to admit that it'd been fun to feel like I was making a difference for someone, even if that person wasn't Brian Nelson. I'd always kind of worried I was only good at training because of the huge crush I'd had on him. Now it seemed that maybe that wasn't true.

At supper that night Dad kept grumbling about how all the asphalt plants were closed, muttering to himself like some sort of crazy neighbor that you'd never visit when you were trick-or-treating. Curtis finally took the bait and asked what he was talking about.

"Jeez, you know what asphalt is. I want the driveway done for Win for Christmas, and you can't do that without asphalt. What the hell are they teaching you, anyway?"

Which got us grinning, because why in the world would Red Bend Middle School teach kids about paving? But all I said was "I'm sure you'll figure something out."

"Yeah. I got Jimmy Ott working on it. We'll get it done."

See, our driveway is just as run down as the rest of our farm, which doesn't matter for our beat-up pickup and our beat-up Caravan, or the milk tankers because those trucks have big tough wheels that can handle our potholes without blinking twice. But Win of course is in a wheelchair, and even if by some miracle he started walking, he still wouldn't be able to navigate from his van to the kitchen. That's why Dad wanted to pave that one area, from the van parking space to our kitchen door, and then build a ramp, a really nice one, into the house. But I guess he hadn't counted on no asphalt.

He'd figure something out, though. He always did. It might not be pretty or last very long, but there was always a solution somewhere. And in the meantime I had a quiz to study for or I'd have my own problems. And then when Mom called I got a whole new set of problems, because Win wanted to hear about my calls, what I'd said to the coaches and they'd said to me, and when he heard how they'd invited me to visit — which is just being polite, how many times have you heard someone say, "Stop by whenever"? — he said I needed to set some trips up PDQ.

"I can't go on trips! I've got games, you know."

Win snorted. "Against who?"

"Cougar Lake and West Lake, and Hawley next week — *Hawley.*"

"You can miss Cougar Lake."

"I can't miss a game!"

He sighed. "You're not going to do this, are you?"

"I can't miss a game, Win."

"Okay then. I will."

"You'll visit?"

"I'll set them up. I'd say the U of M, and Madison . . . Iowa too, they've got a good program —"

I found my voice, finally. "But — what are you talking about? How am I supposed to get to Iowa?"

"We'll figure something out," he said in his super-annoying Win Schwenk way.

I didn't want to say this next thing, but he left me no choice. "Win, you can't even dial."

"They've got a special phone here I can use. I'll make it part of my OT."

Well, what was I supposed to say to *that?* So in the end I agreed, because if nothing else I knew Dad in a million years wouldn't leave his cows to drive me that far, no matter what his firstborn said, and there was no way Mom would ever let me drive it alone.

Tuesday we had a game, and Coach K was on my case non-stop, only guess how well that worked. I ended up fouling out in the third quarter and spent the rest of the game on the bench, thinking that however much Coach K might try, and Win, and Jerry Knudsen might try even, there was no way to get around me being D.J. All of their pressure just made me that much worse.

That night Win was pretty decent about it, all things considered. He'd heard from Dad about the game and didn't give me any grief about blowing it. I guess even he could tell I was upset, or maybe Dad had told him, which meant even Dad could tell, which meant it must have been completely obvious. Win just said I'd done well for being double-teamed and that he'd like to see me play sometime, which was nice to hear even if it wasn't ever going to happen. And then just as we were winding down, he said it was all set for me to visit the U of M on Saturday.

"What?"

"Kathy Ott said she'd be thrilled to drive you. Thrilled," he repeated, in case I'd missed that word. "You can stop by St. Margaret's on the way home. And we're all set up for Madison —"

"St. Margaret's? Madison?"

"Do you have any video of those captain's practices?"

"What?"

He sighed like it was completely my fault I had no idea what he was talking about. "The ones you're holding after practice? That's great stuff. Coaches really like seeing that sort of thing —"

"You mean with Ashley? I helped her one day!"

"But your coach said you two are going to make it a regular thing."

"You talked to Coach K?"

"Yeah," he said, like it was totally obvious. "And you really need to videotape it."

"Do you want some video of my sock drawer as well?" Actually I didn't say this, but I thought it, because video of my socks couldn't be any duller than me coaching Ashley on free throws. "Win . . ."

"You need to let some of the other girls in on those practices too." Like they were begging to join us and I was saying no. "And Kathy will come by Saturday morning, so you better be ready."

After I got off the phone I had to study for A&P, which was especially fun now that I had a trip to Minneapolis hanging over my head. Not that Kathy Ott is bad — she's actually super nice. But the thought that Win had *called* her and asked her to drive me . . . I swear, Win on top of everything else must be some kind of brainwasher. Maybe that's how he gets people to do whatever he wants, like me training all November for him, and Kathy giving up a weekend to drive me around.

But I did study some in the end, enough to do okay on the quiz. And after practice Ashley and I worked more on her defense skills, the cafeteria guys giving us the hairy eyeball because we were screwing up their floor-washing routine, although Coach K supposedly had worked that out, doing his own brainwashing program on them.

Beaner even came by for a bit and played offense while I coached Ashley on guarding. Which was something to see, all right, because Beaner's like two feet taller than she is and every time she got close, guarding him the way she's supposed to with her arms up — as high as she can get them, anyway — he'd poke her in the ribs. Which should have made me mad, Beaner messing with my student like that, but I was too busy laughing and also reassuring Ashley that tickling never happens in a game.

"Maybe, you know, I should tickle someone else," Beaner said, eyeing me with that boyfriend smile he does so well, and I opened my mouth to shoot back a response but nothing came out because all the thinking blood had rushed to my ears instead, and my bright red cheeks. And he came after me, but I move pretty fast when I'm being chased, even when I'm blushing, and then he had to go back to practice. Although it took about half an hour for my insides to calm down from all his flirting. And about the same amount of time to convince Ashley to lift her arms again, she was so spooked, but she did in the end, and you know, she was playing so much better — not as in *Let's get out the video camera*, but at least I came away feeling I was actually good at something.

Maybe I could end up as one of those local guys who helps out with coaching. Take a whole team of Ashleys and turn them into short genius players, like something in a movie. Maybe Beaner and I could do it together. And all those short genius players would figure out fancy physics tricks with the ball, develop shots no one had thought of ever before, and we'd win all our games.

"Whatcha thinking about?" Curtis asked out of the blue on the ride home, as I was going over that genius hoops dream team in my mind.

I jumped, which made us both laugh. "Nothing. Basketball."

"Roger that," Curtis said. Which shouldn't have made us crack up, but it did.

We pulled in next to Jimmy Ott's Explorer, which cheered me up even more, because we all like Jimmy Ott so much, as much as we like his wife. Dad had done a great job of plowing the yard and he'd even shoveled out Win's special parking space, I guess to show Jimmy.

"Roger that, over and out," I was saying to Curtis as we trooped inside, stomping the snow off our boots. Then I stopped dead.

Curtis banged into me. "Hey!" he said, and then he stopped too, because it wasn't just Jimmy at the table, drinking coffee and eating some sort of coffee cake that made the kitchen smell amazing, especially if you've just finished three hours of basketball. There was this other man who looked so handsome and also so familiar that for a minute I knew we had a movie star in our house. I couldn't quite come up with his name, but it had to be one of them.

The man stood up. "Well, hello at last. I'm Dan Nelson."

"Oh," I said, shaking his hand as I tried to figure out what I'd seen Dan Nelson in.

Jimmy Ott grinned at my confusion. "This here's Brian Nelson's dad."

"Oh," I said again, in a very different voice. We were still shaking hands, but I couldn't get my brain to figure out how to stop. "Um . . . pleased to meet you."

"The pleasure's mine. Brian spent so much time describing all your other qualities that he never mentioned how pretty you are."

Behind me Curtis made a choking sound. I spun around — we were done shaking hands, finally — and there he was looking so innocent that the veins were sticking out on his neck.

Dad eyed him. "You say hello to Mr. Nelson, son?"

"Hey," said Curtis. Even the veins on the back of his neck were sticking out. It was a wonder he could speak at all. Although he did sound kind of strangled.

"D.J. here's running double practices at the high school," Dad said like he was fit to burst. How the heck did he know about Ashley? Was Coach K publishing a newsletter on me or something?

"I believe it," Brian's dad said. "This girl's quite a miracle worker, from what I hear."

I shuffled. "Yeah, um . . . We should shower."

Jimmy gave me a pat. "Good to see you again, D.J. George, this is one heck of a coffee cake."

Mr. Nelson turned back to their conversation. "I'm sure the guy could rustle up some asphalt. He's done it for me a couple times . . ."

Halfway up the stairs Curtis muttered, real quietly so only I could hear, "He didn't mention you were so pretty."

I swung at him but he danced out of the way. "How's *Sarah* doing?" I shot back.

"She's fine. At least *her* parents don't flirt with me." He lunged for the bathroom and slammed the door one step ahead of me so I crashed into it with a huge bang, not to mention my kicking it as well.

I sat on the bed in a cloud of D.J. stink for I don't know how long, trying to figure this out. What the heck was Mr. Nelson doing in our kitchen? Not four months ago he'd been all set to sue Red Bend about me playing football — he'd done everything he could to talk Brian out of working for us — and now here he was eating Dad's coffee cake. I mean, he did get Win that van. And Brian had said, in the one conversation we'd had since we stopped talking, that doing that had made him awfully happy. Which is nice, frankly, that you can do such a good deed and get satisfaction from it. But I'd thought Mr. Nelson was just being nice out of guilt or something, because he was so relieved it wasn't his son all crippled up. Or happy I wasn't seeing Brian anymore.

Not that I'm objecting to his generosity. But it's one thing to be all generous just through the company you own, and another to sit at our kitchen table shooting the breeze. Why would a rich, handsome guy like Mr. Nelson do that?

Curtis finished finally, and I took as long a shower as I could, thinking the whole time about Brian. What would Brian think about his dad's whole baloney about me being pretty? His dad did own a car dealership. Maybe if you sell cars for a living, that's just the way you talk. Although I couldn't help but grin at the thought of Brian's reaction to his dad getting so cheesy with me. It'd almost be worth having him here for just a moment, just so he and I could share a grin about our totally mortifying fathers.

I could even tell Brian that I'd thought his father was a movie star, which would absolutely crack him up. I wouldn't even have to tell him not to tell anyone, because that's not the kind of guy Brian is. Though even if he did, you know, it wouldn't be so bad. I mean, if Mr. Nelson was going to all the trouble of helping us with our driveway and everything, the least he could get was a compliment in return.

Brian would love my Ashley genius b-ball team, too. He'd suggest some genius plays no one had ever thought up, or some genius players. He'd probably even have some advice on how I could help Ashley out more, help her out with college . . .

I was so busy thinking about Brian and all the great conversations we could have if we were still having conversations that I almost froze to death when the hot water ran out. I had to do one of those superfast dry-offs and quick yank on my sweatpants and Red Bend hoops T-shirt, which are *not* pajamas even though I sleep in them, only I'd forgotten my slippers and could feel the cold oozing into my toes from the bathroom floor, and then from my bedroom floor because my slippers weren't there either. Curtis was downstairs playing with Smut — you could hear her growling up a storm with her tug-of-war voice. I hollered down for him to toss them up, but Curtis fakes deafness better than anyone I know. I could either stand at the top of the stairs all evening hollering my lungs out, or just get them myself and get on with life, and my homework.

"Did you even hear me?" I asked as I dashed into the kitchen, still having to holler over Smut's tug-of-war growls as the two of them duked it out behind the table. "All I needed was my stupid — Oh my God!"

Because it turned out Smut wasn't playing tug of war with Curtis after all. She was playing with Brian Nelson.

"No, it's Brian," he said, dropping the rope at once. "Remember . . . ? That was a joke — ow!" Because Smut, fed up with waiting for him, snapped her rope around and caught him right in the jaw.

"Smut!" I cried out. And then, "What are you doing here?"

Brian stood up, rubbing his chin. "I had to pick up my dad, you know, and I asked if I could, you know, say hey. They're out looking at the driveway." A long pause. "So . . . hey."

"Hey." I'd forgotten completely about the slippers. My feet could have been two blocks of ice and I wouldn't have noticed.

"That was really good coffee cake," he put in. Smut thwacked him in the knee with her rope, just a little reminder he still had a game to play, but he ignored her. "I saved you a piece. Your dad said I could finish it, but, you know . . ."

Now I saw the pan sitting there on the table. "Thanks," I said. I broke the last piece in half. "You want some?"

"Some more, you mean?" He smiled and held out his hand. "If you don't mind. I mean, it's really . . ."

"Just when you thought you'd recovered from Schwenk cooking."

Brian laughed. "Oh, please. You have no idea. I would eat here every night — seriously. My mom could burn water. And my dad . . ."

"I've got to say, seeing him sitting at that table . . . I had no clue who it was."

Brian laughed even more. "I know! I was like, 'You're going *where?*' And he was being all cool about it, like it was no big deal . . . We should have gotten him to help with haying."

I cracked up, almost choking on the last of the coffee cake. I was at the poking-at-crumbs-with-my-finger stage, not yet ready to say it was kicked. "Can you imagine? I don't think he'd have been very happy about it."

"He'd say it would give him a heart attack or something, that he'd hurt himself . . . Although the guy is a total klutz. He broke his wrist, you know, planting an apple tree."

"A *tree?* How do you break your wrist planting a tree?"

"Beats me. It was a real little one, too. A couple weeks ago I called him Johnny Appleseed, just as a joke, and I thought he was going to blow a gasket . . ." Brian ducked to scratch Smut behind her ears, Smut eating it up because she loves Brian so much. All of a sudden he wouldn't look at me. "You know . . . something like that will happen, some little funny thing like that, and every single time I'll think *I can't wait to tell D.J.* And then I'll remember we're not talking anymore, and I'll be so freaking bummed. Three or four times a day."

"Me too," I said. No longer jabbing at cake crumbs.

"It's like half of me is missing. You know?"

I nodded.

"I'm so sorry for the way I treated you. Man, you must hate my guts. I hate my guts just thinking about it."

"That's okay." Jeepers, D.J. You could run me over with a school bus and the first thing I'd say probably, lying there in a puddle of blood and little bones, is *That's okay.*

He was still scratching Smut, scowling to himself. "No, it's not."

All of a sudden it hit me: He was right. It wasn't. And more than that, right now Brian was doing that thing he's so good at, the thing he's the very best at, which is talking. Using words to take away what he'd done. What he'd done with his actions.

"You hurt me so much." I didn't realize at first I'd said this aloud — isn't that funny? It just popped out without my even knowing.

"I know. I'm sorry. I know you don't believe me, not yet, but I'm going to . . . It's not going to be the same."

I looked at him — I'd been real busy staring at the kitchen floor, memorizing patterns I already knew by heart — but now I looked him right in the eye. "You're right. I don't believe you."

"I *miss* you —"

"Yeah. I miss you too." I gulped. All of a sudden it was all I could do not to lose it.

An engine started up outside. The guys must have finished their driveway powwow.

Brian took a step toward me, looking as miserable as I felt. "I'm sorry."

"I know," I whispered. I squeaked, actually, because it took so much effort not to cry.

"Yo! Brian!" Mr. Nelson called. Through the kitchen window we could see him in Mr. Ott's headlights, waving to us.

"I've got to go," Brian said. "I'm sorry." He smiled at me from the doorway, then shut the door really softly behind him.

Smut watched him go, still holding her rope, her tail wagging slower and slower until it drooped to a stop. She let go of her rope with a sigh.

"Those are words," I whispered. "Those are just words."

Dad was heading inside, I could see, and all of a sudden I couldn't get out of the kitchen fast enough. I made it all the way upstairs and into my room before the back door even opened. Then, alone at last, I dropped onto my bed and sobbed.

7
TRAVELING

HERE'S ONE FOR THE RECORD BOOKS: our game Friday against Cougar Lake got canceled on account of lice.

Seriously.

Friday morning Beaner stuck his head into English to announce it, grinning like crazy.

"Lice?" Mrs. Stolze asked, touching her hair. It's really hard to hear the word and not do that.

"Yeah. So it's just afternoon practice instead. Hey, D.J., wanna go to the movies tonight?"

I'm surprised blood didn't start spurting out of my eyeballs, I blushed so hard. Everyone laughed. Although Kayla and Brittany and about four boy players are in that class too, so maybe they were laughing about Cougar Lake instead. Maybe.

I shrugged in what I hoped was a normal teen girl way. "Sure."

"Awesome. I'll pick you up at your place. Rock on, Mrs. Stolze." And he galloped off.

Did you see that? Beaner had no trouble asking me out —
in front of a whole roomful of people! See the difference between him and Brian? If I was that kind of person, I'd take a
video of Beaner and send it to Brian just to show him how
some guys treat me. But I'm not that mean. Also I have no
idea how to take videos. Also no equipment to take them
with. And also I wasn't going to even *think* about Brian, not
ever, ever again. So video was out.

Anyway, thanks to Cougar Lake we had a regular practice,
but with fun stuff like dribbling blindfolded. Coach K gave us
a little talk about how anyone can get lice and we shouldn't
hold it against them, and we all nodded like grownups but inside we were thinking it'd be a while yet before Cougar Lake
heard the end of it. And Ashley and I spent time afterward on
her squaring up, getting her body facing the right way when
she passed, which was especially tough given how hard it is
for her to figure out how her body parts work or where the
various parts even are.

There were two pickup trucks in the yard when I got
home, a real one with scratches and toolboxes and lumber,
and the other a shiny new tricked-out ride. A couple guys in
parkas and tool belts were hammering away outside the
kitchen door, building an actual wheelchair ramp out of new
wood with nonslip patches and a handrail and everything,
nothing like what Dad would have made out of leftover ply-
wood and roofing nails. They nodded to me in that way

worker guys do, and because I didn't want to bother them I stomped through the snow to the front door, trying not to get snow in my shoes. When I opened the door, this amazing smell of chili hit me, Dad's buffalo meat chili — seriously, it's real buffalo meat, which is pretty trippy to think about — which he keeps working on, each time making it better than it already is. And sitting there at the kitchen table, a beer in one hand, was Mr. Nelson.

That explained it. Because it's not like worker guys had ever been to our place before — for a moment I'd thought I was at the wrong house, even, when I first pulled in. They were with Mr. Nelson, part of his Schwenk family charity project.

"Hey there, sport, where you been?" Dad asked, stirring away, a beer in his other hand.

"Practice. Game got canceled," I said. Wondering what Brian had told Mr. Johnny Appleseed Nelson about me.

But he didn't seem to be thinking anything, or at least nothing bad. "No kidding. Why?"

"Lice," I said. Like it was nothing. "I'm going out tonight, okay?"

"Sure," said Dad. "So anyway, Dan, the co-op's been around twenty-some years, and the biggest farm's got over two hundred head." And Mr. Nelson actually looked interested. Who *was* this guy?

⑨ ⑨ ⑨ ⑨ ⑨

I didn't have much time to think about Mr. Nelson even if I wanted to, or about Brian (although thanks to his visit I was now suffocating in Brian memories), because I had this other problem called what to wear on my date with Beaner. In the end I settled on jeans and a Red Bend sweatshirt — real exciting choices there, D.J. — and did a teeny bit more work on my hair than I normally would, and even put on some lipstick I found on Mom's dresser. Maybe Beaner would bring his little sister along and she could pick something out.

Dad and Mr. Nelson were digging in to the chili as I came downstairs. "Don't worry, I'll just send Brian over to help," Mr. Nelson was saying.

I froze, one foot in midair.

But right then there was a knock at the door. Dad hollered it was open, and Beaner came bouncing in. "Hey! That's some awesome ramp out there. You guys totally need a skateboard."

"Um, hey, Beaner," I managed. Had Mr. Nelson really just said he was going to send Brian over? "This is my dad, and, ah, a friend of the family —"

"Dan Nelson." Mr. Nelson shook Beaner's hand. "So what are you two kids up to tonight?"

I turned red, but Beaner just laughed. "I dunno. Burn the school down, cause a riot . . . What were you thinking, D.J.?"

"Um . . . something like that."

"You drive safe with my little girl, you hear me?" Dad said.

Which made me turn twice as red — jeez, Dad, could you be more embarrassing? This would probably end up being my last date ever.

But Beaner just said that he would, and he even helped me put on my coat, which made me blush even more, while Dad explained to Mr. Nelson how I was going to the U of M the next day to check out their basketball program, bragging about me while I had to listen, and then off Beaner and I went.

I'll confess — just to be totally honest here — that I actually didn't mind so much having Mr. Nelson of all people watch me go off on a date with a guy, a guy as confident and relaxed and tall as Beaner is. Not that Beaner can help being tall, but still. And thinking Mr. Nelson might go home and report to Brian that I was seeing someone. That was okay, the notion of Brian chewing on that one. Especially considering the lovely chat the two of us had just had.

Although I wasn't supposed to be thinking about Brian!

I especially wasn't supposed to be thinking about him as I was riding along next to Beaner. But luckily Beaner didn't notice. He was singing away with the car stereo, drumming on the steering wheel and generally being his happy Beaner self. " 'Not to put too fine a point on it, say I'm the only bee in your bonnet . . .' " he sang, squinting his eyes. "What, you don't know these guys?"

"Uh, no." Which wasn't too tough an answer seeing as I don't know anything when it comes to music. And I'm not just being modest when I say that.

"They're so awesome. My stepdad turned me on to them. 'Bluebird of friendliness . . . like guardian angels it's . . . always near.' "

"What does that even mean?"

"No idea. But it's totally cool." Beaner fast-forwarded. "Check out this one: 'The — sun — is a mass — of in-can-des-cent gas, a gi-gan-tic nu-cle-ar fur-nace . . .' " He was totally into it, lecturing me with finger as he sang. I couldn't help cracking up — you'd have to be dead not to. And he taught me the words so we could "sing a duet" as he put it, although I was laughing way too much to manage singing even if I could sing, which I can't.

Going to the movies is pretty much the only thing you can do in Red Bend until you're legal, so of course the place was packed. Beaner kept his arm around me once we were seated, which I liked, but then he wanted to make out. Which, I know, I've watched millions of kids do. But still. Maybe that was the problem, that I couldn't get out of my head how I used to be one of watchers, Amber whispering jokes about them until I snarfed my popcorn. At least I didn't have to worry about Amber seeing me because she'd gone with Dale to St. Paul. But what if they hadn't? What if the two of them were here? Imagine how stressful *that* would be . . . Plus I actually kind of wanted to watch the movie. Luckily it got pretty exciting after a while — onscreen, I mean — and we kind of forgot to do anything else.

Afterward we hung out with a bunch of ball players at Taco Bell, chatting about the movie and making fun of Cougar Lake lice even though we shouldn't. I didn't say too much — big surprise there — but my mind was going about a million miles an hour, checking all the time to make sure I wasn't doing anything embarrassing, and then checking the other tables to see if anyone was looking at me funny, and then whenever someone asked me a question being extra careful to make my answer acceptable, you know, before I opened my mouth. Which put a brake, an even bigger brake, on my talking.

Was this what it was like hanging out with cool kids? Was it always this much pressure? No one else seemed stressed at all. So maybe it was just my insaneness. Plus I couldn't help but remember that time this fall when I'd been in Taco Bell — with Beaner, interestingly — and Brian saw me and ran away before I ruined his life by saying hello to him in front of his friends.

Well, at least Beaner didn't mind my presence. He didn't even hassle me for sitting there like a big old lump, and he told everyone how good my house smells and how they all had to figure out a way to come over just to get a whiff of that chili.

"You know, we could hold hoops practice in your drive-way," he said.

"In the snow?" I asked, and a couple kids laughed.

"Oh, totally. Be all like, 'He shoots! His gloves connect! A snowball knocks it off the rim!' It could be like basketball and a huge snowball fight put together!"

Which got us all on a huge discussion of *that*, and what an intentional foul would be, and when I suggested that the refs could be snowmen everyone laughed even more. And then on the way home Beaner and I made out in the car a bit, which was okay except he was really into it, a little too much, and I had to slow him down.

Lying in bed that night, I almost started crying. Who knew a date would be so much work? It was never like that when I went out with Amber, hanging out with her at Taco Bell. That was just fun. And sure, I'd laughed tonight, and even cracked a couple jokes. But I was just so aware every second of what I was doing and how I was acting. Worrying I wasn't doing it right. Is this what being popular meant? Getting ulcers? Instead of being a background nobody with Amber?

Maybe Brian had been smart to stay away from me in public. Maybe he understood me better that I'd even thought. Maybe he'd been right after all.

You know how the Red Bend ladies had been in a flutter because they wanted to help our Schwenk Family Tragedy but didn't know how? Well, apparently they decided that the least they could do was clean. So Saturday morning three ladies showed up with brooms and vacuums and spray bottles — showed up while Curtis was still in bed, which must have been a shock — and set to work scrubbing and washing and taking care of stuff. This was especially great news for me, because Dad and Curtis had kind of counted on me doing all that work, I guess because I have ovaries, but it's not like the thrill of laundry gets me up every morning. So that was awesome. But Curtis didn't look too pleased about getting tossed out of bed so Cindy Jorgensen could wash his sheets. And Dad was fit to be tied over what they did to his frying pan because apparently he'd been treating it some special way and the ladies scrubbed it so there wasn't any grease left in it at all, which you'd think would be a good thing but Dad seemed to feel the opposite. Although I noticed he didn't complain to *them,* so I guess he didn't mind so much having clean underwear again.

Then Kathy Ott showed up with a big cup of coffee, all perky and chatty and ready to go. Win must have done some kind of brainwashing job on her. You'd have thought she'd won a trip to Disney World or something, the way she carried on about getting to escort me to Minnesota in her nice new Subaru with its clean carpeting and unscuffed dashboard that no kid had ever put their feet on.

In Minneapolis, which we found without too much trouble at all, we met that nice lady coach and my University of

Minnesota student escort, who just happened to be my buddy Tyrona. Normally on these types of visits they take you to Mall of America, which is obviously a really huge draw seeing as it's the biggest mall *in* America. But I didn't have any money, and also I'd been there with Brian and didn't want to spend any more time being reminded of him. So I asked Tyrona if we could do something basketball-ish instead. I couldn't play or anything — the NCAA would totally spaz about *that* — but I wouldn't mind watching. Anyway, it turned out that this weekend her old school was holding a tournament! It was like the perfect solution.

So we got there, taking the bus, which was a huge adventure in and of itself for a hick like me, and then when I saw her high school gym I must have looked like a hick times ten, standing there with my mouth hanging open. The building was big enough to hold all of Red Bend. The people *and* the houses. And maybe even the cows.

Tyrona cracked up. "You've never been here?"

"Why would I?"

"They hold some AAU tournaments here."

"What's that?" I said without thinking.

"AAU?" Tyrona frowned at me. "You don't know AAU? How do you play in the summer?"

"I, uh, I don't play in the summer."

Tyrona turned me around, studying my face like she was a teacher and I was a student she didn't quite get. "You don't play summer ball."

"We have to farm."

"You have to farm."

"I know I should — I will next summer . . . Um, how bad is it? That I don't play."

"It's no big deal. Coach found you without it, so it can't be that bad."

But — obviously — it was.

And then the game started and I found out why. Because those girls were *good*. They talked back to the refs just like on TV, and two girls got in a fight right on the court — not that that's good, but at least it shows how tough they are, aggressive in a way that I'll never be. It was pretty intimidating, I have to say. Although it helped that Tyrona pointed out how the coach kept yelling at one girl to pass but she kept trying these three-pointers that kept getting intercepted. Finally he benched her. That perked me up a bit, because whatever I am in basketball, it's certainly not that dumb.

Plus Tyrona kept telling me how great it would be if I played for the U of M — even though she's never seen me play! But she said Bill brags about me all the time, and so does Aaron, his roommate, which made my ears go bright pink I'm sure. And it was awesome to talk hoops with her, especially because there wasn't any of the "that's good for a girl" garbage you get sometimes when you try to talk hoops with guys.

Speaking of which, we even got on the subject of guys, and I told her about Beaner, how much fun he is and how good at one-on-one, how he can steal but I can shoot so we're pretty evenly matched. She said she was totally jealous and that I needed to bring a bunch of guys like him with me when I came. Then she asked about the other guy — I had told her about Brian when I met her last time — and I shrugged and said we weren't really talking anymore.

"Sounds like you got something a lot better now," she said. "Guys like Brian, they need a lot of time to grow up. Too much time, sometimes."

So all in all, it was a pretty fantastic afternoon. And then that night Kathy and I watched Tyrona and the rest of them play Wisconsin, which is a big rivalry and of course Wisconsin was also on my list, so this was a chance to see them too.

College players are so amazing! My jaw was on the floor at how fast they moved, and how *much*. It's like they never stop even for a second, like a bunch of gnats that always know where they're going and are all my size. And the arena was so large — the Barn, they call it, although I can't imagine keeping anything in a barn that size except maybe dinosaurs — and so loud you could barely hear yourself think. Tyrona was playing really well — they all were — and I have to admit that it was a rush to think about *me* out there in front of ten thousand screaming people, a million more watching on TV, and my picture in a nice shiny book. Not that I'm a fan of having my picture taken, but the U of M folks do a really nice job of it. Tyrona looks even prettier there than she does in real life. Being at that game was like realizing I might have a winning lottery ticket after all.

Which shows how good Win is at brainwashing. I actually spent the game thinking I could play Big Ten ball. I was a hard worker, after all. I could play almost as well as some of the girls on the court, even though I was four or five years younger and didn't practice twenty hours a week like you do in D-I. With that sort of experience, I could really be something . . .

Except. Except I'd forgotten to factor in one thing while I was sitting there making a big stuck-up list of all the stuff I was good at. I forgot to factor in *me*. And when I said that I watched that whole game feeling good about myself, I forgot to add "until the end."

Because in the last twenty seconds they were tied. Then Wisconsin made a three-pointer. They both called time-outs, and then it was down to the last seven seconds. Tyrona made this totally amazing interception and raced downcourt for a lay-up that she also made, and on top of that she got fouled, which meant she got to stand at the free-throw line — just like everyone does, just like I do, bouncing the ball and saying a little free-throw chant — while eight thousand Minnesota fans cheered and two thousand Wisconsin fans screamed and booed and waved their arms and did everything they could to make her miss.

It was the most intense moment I've ever seen. In basketball, and in life. Because I was there for one thing instead of watching it on TV, which would be like watching from another planet compared to this. And it was so loud. Loud like you can't even imagine. The whole game rested on these two shots! This huge school rivalry, and all these fans who'd paid money for tickets and gone out on a cold Saturday night, driving all the way to Minneapolis, or taking the bus, and they were all expecting Tyrona to perform. To make it.

Looking around the Barn, my heart stopped. It might as well have been me out there on the free-throw line, all these people waiting for me to win the game for them. My hands started sweating and my mouth went dry, and I had to close my eyes so I didn't see Tyrona take her first shot. But I heard the enormous groan, and the screaming from the Wisconsin side, and I knew she'd missed.

I forced my eyes open because I had to be there for her second shot. I watched her face as closely as I've ever watched anything. Saw her whisper her little thing, and pluck at her jersey and touch the cross at her neck, and then set her jaw, and shoot.

And miss. Again.

The Wisconsin fans started shrieking, and all the Wisconsin players pounded onto the court while eight thousand Minnesota fans just sat there. Some of the little kids were crying.

Tyrona had made kids cry. She'd blown it, and Minnesota lost. It wasn't *her* fault, I know that; it's everyone on the team who wins and everyone who loses. The other Minnesota players crowded around Tyrona who was crying, which she had every right to do, and you could tell they were all saying just the kind of things I'd say in that situation if I was there, and that their words weren't helping any more than mine would have.

All of a sudden I had to put my head between my knees. I never in my life want eight thousand people disappointed in me like that, yelling and booing and crying. I mean, look at me. Look how freaked out I got when Jerry Knudsen from freaking Ibsen College watched me play! Look how freaked I got just sitting in Taco Bell!

Kathy Ott leaned over and squeezed my knee. "You okay?"

I nodded. I felt too sick to argue.

"It can be pretty brutal out there." Which she should know as much as anyone, being married to a football coach. "Are you going to be okay with this?"

"Yeah," I said.

And you know what? I was.

8
THERE'S NO NEED TO PANIC, BECAUSE EVERYTHING'S GOING TO WORK OUT FINE

IT TOOK ME A WHILE, I'll admit. I spent a bunch of hours that night staring into the darkness. But I made my peace, finally, with this whole situation. And this is what I realized: Division I is not for me.

The next day we stopped by St. Margaret's College, which has a really pretty campus with no ugly buildings at all, and a gym that's as new and big as Hawley's, and I paid extra-close attention to the coach, who because of Win's brainwashing had made a special trip in on Sunday just for me, and everything I saw I liked. I'd probably be the star player, but that's not a bad thing. I might even get to play against the U of M, in money games that would get the school a new floor or a building or a private plane, and if I didn't lose my head I might even make my free throws and get a taste of what it was like to be booed and cheered by ten thousand people. That's all I needed. Just a taste. And it wouldn't matter if we lost so long as I played well, which of course I'd try my best to do, and I wouldn't ever feel guilty about the score.

Sure, Bill played Big Ten, and Win PAC-Ten, but my brothers aren't me. Which is pretty obvious, but it's still worth pointing out. And pointing out that they weren't the ones who spent all summer managing the farm while Dad had surgery. They were off at fancy football camps. Maybe the same thing in my brain that made me too wimpy — if you want to call it that — to play D-I, maybe it's the same thing that saved the farm. Because everyone has bad and good in them all at once, the way Ashley Erdel is both bad at basketball and good at school, and maybe for the very same reasons.

When Win called Sunday night, I didn't even get rattled. Because that's just the way his brain works, getting so caught up in sports and competition and being the absolute best competitor you can be, and until he got a real job I was just going to have to put up with it as best I could. So I said the visits were very nice and I really liked St. Margaret's, and I didn't even get defensive when he started ragging on it, and I let him blab away about how I still needed to take video and just kept nodding and saying okay, staying cool with my new inner peace.

Beaner called too, to say he'd seen me in the audience on TV, only for a second but he knew it was me, and he was so psyched that he knew someone *on television,* even for something as little as that. He was totally impressed when he found out I knew Tyrona, and he agreed those last two shots had completely sucked.

"It'll be so awesome, you know, to watch you in college," he said, and I laughed and said it would be. Because he didn't specify what it was exactly he'd be watching me doing, and as far as I was concerned, it would be just as awesome to have Beaner watch me sitting in the bleachers, or playing a money game that we lose by eighty.

And Monday during lunch, I called the U of M just like Win had told me to, thanking them for the weekend. I couldn't say, "I'm sorry but there's no way I can play Big Ten ball," because sure as shooting that would get back to Win. But I did a great job of making it clear indirectly, asking how many other girls they were looking at, saying how bad I felt for Tyrona and how I'd never in my life want to be in that position. The coach kind of chuckled and agreed that no one wants that, but she got my point. Recruiting is like a board game where one side creeps forward and then the other side does, no one willing to give too much away. By saying all that, I'd moved myself three spaces back. Which made me even more relaxed and peaceful.

All this, weird as it sounds, made me a better player. I guess because I didn't feel so much pressure anymore, so much belly-knot fear that I wouldn't measure up. Now that I didn't even want to measure up, the coast was clear for me just to be me. So when we played Prophetstown on Tuesday, I actually kept my head a bit. It wasn't like I was hollering up and down the court, but I didn't freak when Coach K started riding me. And a couple times when I saw something that was totally obvious, I had smarts enough to whisper it to Kari. We did an especially good job on this play where I draw two defenders while Kayla drives in. That worked five or six times, and Prophetstown never seemed to figure it out.

We won, which was important because winning is important, duh, no matter what any grownup tells you, but also because we had Hawley coming up on Friday. And Hawley's no Prophetstown. They're more like the Los Angeles Lakers. Which Coach K reminded us afterward, how hard our next game was going to be. Looking straight at Ashley, he mentioned how much a couple players were improving, and she just about smiled her face off, hearing this. Then he said that anyone who wanted to could join Ashley and D.J.'s little practices if it was okay with the two of us. Which I'll confess was a kick to hear, because if nothing else it meant he thought I wasn't doing so bad.

I couldn't help wondering a couple times whether Brian would come to Friday's game. Which was stupid of me, particularly given that huge kitchen talk we'd had. But I didn't have time to sit around mooning over Brian; I had too much else going on. First of all, Mom was calling every night to ask how we were coming on decorating for Christmas, even though this year it felt like the holiday spirit had slipped past our house without even stopping in for a visit. Dad kept telling her we'd be ready for her and Win's arrival, which at least meant I wasn't the only one procrastinating. Which was good, given that my life was also extremely full of this little thing called school, a history quiz and a big English paper on *another* extremely depressing book — would it kill the teachers to assign us just one book, once, that didn't make you want to jump off a cliff? And a big midterm in math, which automatically causes the jumping.

I got through it all, more or less, and then the last afternoon before break, we had a pep rally. It was a typical thing, the gym full of kids and balloons and our not-so-great pep band, Mr. Slutsky announcing the girls' basketball team one by one. Only just after he'd said the last girl, a bunch of kids started laughing and pointing like crazy, and I turned around to see Beaner coming out of the boys' locker room dressed . . . well, it was something. He was wearing a big T-shirt with HAWLEY 00 written with Sharpie on the front, and long b-ball shorts like girls wear, and b-ball shoes. But he was also wearing a big girly wig, and lots of makeup that he'd clearly put on himself, and fake boobs.

He strutted around pushing up his hair, acting like he didn't even notice everyone laughing at him, looking the girl players up and down like they weren't worth his attention. Then he came to me and glared at me with his hands on his hips. The kids in the bleachers were screaming things like "Get him, D.J.!" and "Get her, D.J.!" because it wasn't clear which one of those Beaner was, a him or a her. Then he started these karate moves on me, all these different poses that would make a real karate expert barf.

What was I supposed to do? It was funny, sure, funny as heck. But it was also totally embarrassing, all the kids screaming like that, and calling my name. Beaner was born to draw attention to himself, but unless I'm holding a basketball I don't want to hear my name screamed out, ever. Finally, my face all red even though I was laughing, I made one little gesture, a push like you'd use to move a defender away. Didn't even touch him. But apparently that was enough, because he collapsed on the gym floor with all this arm waving and moaning, twitching like a bug does when you spray it with bug spray, and then lay still.

That was the cue, I guess, for the cheerleaders to start in with "Beat Hawley! Beat Hawley! Beat Hawley!" until everyone in the gym was chanting, even Beaner, who got up and danced around with the cheerleaders, totally hamming it up. Then the boys' team came out and Beaner went and joined *them*, flirting away . . . I wasn't sure any of the boys would even be able to play that night, they were laughing so hard. But by the end of the pep rally everyone in the school, even the kids who are too cool for pep rallies, everyone was absolutely united about beating Hawley.

If Beaner doesn't play hoops in college, he should definitely try out for the school mascot, because he'd be better at that job than anyone I know, and would end up on TV as much as most of the players. And I'd watch every game just to see him in action.

After school we didn't have practice, just a little review and a bit of drilling because Coach wanted us fresh for the night, so I got to watch Curtis play *his* game, his middle school game, against Hawley's middle school. Actually Beaner and I went together with Abby, his little sister who was so psyched to be with us, both of them doing these dance moves whenever Red Bend scored. It made me love Beaner so much — not I-want-to-marry-you love, but the you-are-so-wonderful-and-it's-great-hanging-out-with-you kind. Just like he'd promised, Beaner even programmed my cheap little cell phone with that Elvis ring tone. I couldn't help noticing how appropriate the song was for him. "A little less conversation, a little more action": that was Beaner. And Beaner's kind of action *was* satisfactioning me — that's how Elvis phrased it, although I suspect he was referring to a different action than cheering eighth grade basketball players. But you never know.

Plus Curtis had a great game, which isn't hard when you're 6'2" and have years of practice shooting hoops in our driveway. I have to say, our potholes sure teach you how to scramble after bad passes, which comes in pretty handy when you're playing with a bunch of gawky middle-schoolers. Or gawky high-schoolers for that matter.

⑨ ⑨ ⑨ ⑨

All week we'd been watching game tapes of Hawley, Coach K showing us their moves and their two best players: 23, who's a center and a real bruiser, and this 11, who's little and scrappy and clearly a big problem. I never like watching other teams' tapes — I always feel like I'm cheating even though I remind myself that sure as shooting they're watching tapes of us, that probably right at this minute a coach somewhere is pointing out Red Bend's 12 and how she'll need to be double-teamed. Then I don't feel so bad. And we had some new plays all worked out, including that one where I draw defense so Kayla can score. At least with Kayla we had our own little scrappy player.

The game — well, it was really loud, which I think you can imagine. Hawley has a much bigger gym than we do, bigger and newer and nicer because everything in Hawley is bigger and newer and nicer and I wouldn't be surprised if they built the gym just to rub that in our faces. Not that I'm bitter. About half of Red Bend was there, including Dad and Curtis and even Amber and Dale, who for once stayed in town for the weekend just to watch, which I really appreciated. And Mr. Jorgensen was videotaping it. I always feel bad that Mr. and Mrs. Jorgensen have to split up to watch Kari and Kyle play, but that's how it works around here. One team goes to the other school and their other team comes to ours, so boys and girls are playing at the same time in different places because no one's thought up a better solution to watching boys and girls both.

In case you're wondering, the game was extremely physical. That 23 was a total — well, the term female dog comes to mind. Just as mean as she could be. And guess who got to guard her? Luckily I had a couple things going for me, like the fact that I grew up playing with guys who've never paid much attention to pain, theirs or anyone else's. And I'd seen how physical the U of M players get — they practice against guys even. And I've been told I have very sharp elbows. Which shouldn't make me proud, but it does.

Anyway, 23 learned pretty early in the game that anything she dished out, I'd dish right back. She kept fouling me — three times in the first half! And each time I made my free throws. So by the end of the half, she was so mad she was pinching. Which didn't bother me much because I must have the same *Pain? So what?* thing as my brothers.

Yeah, it was pretty ugly.

We were only down by a couple points at the half. Coach K was totally psyched, twirling his pen so hard that I was afraid it was going to go sailing up into space and start orbiting the planet. He was a little too psyched, actually, the way he gets sometimes. He'd even screamed at the refs over a couple bad calls. The calls *were* bad, don't get me wrong, but it's not like a ref ever says, "Whoopsie, I made a mistake — lemme just change that." Yelling just makes them madder. We were going to get a technical if he didn't watch it.

All through halftime I worried about this, and then I thought of Ashley. Our little genius benchwarmer. As we were heading back into the gym, I came up beside her. "Listen," I whispered in her ear, "you need to take care of Coach. If he starts to blow his top, you get on him. Hear me?"

"M-me?"

"*You.* Be aggressive. Be even more aggressive than when you're defending."

Ashley looked like she'd rather play Hawley five-on-one than take this job. But we were already on the court and she didn't have time to argue.

Two minutes in, sure enough, Kari got called for an over-the-back foul even though she was totally vertical. Coach K started screaming, and I jabbed my finger at poor Ashley — I was pretty caught up myself, I guess — to *sit him down.* She kind of tiptoed over and said something, I don't know what, but it worked because he did stop, and sat down, and he even gave her a pat. Which was good to see, because I had enough to worry about without having to babysit my own coach.

Remember how at Tuesday's game I'd whispered things to Kari? Well, it had worked so well that now I tried it again, getting her to call a play with Kayla, which she hollered so loud you could probably hear it at the top of the bleachers, and it worked like a charm. And once I even suggested we switch positions so Kari could get in some of the rebounding she's so good at. And that worked too!

I ended up fouling out with fifteen seconds left, but it was totally worth it because 23 missed both her free throws. Just like Tyrona, only not at all because it was Hawley. And *man* you should have heard Red Bend's reaction. Then Kari rebounded and scored, and we won.

Which meant we all got to run screaming onto the court, everyone from me down to Ashley, and scream twice as loud because it was Hawley's gym we were screaming in, and rub each other's hair and jump up and down and generally celebrate in that way that feels so good when you're doing it and sucks so much when you're watching from the losing side.

Some families came out on the court as well, checking their shoes first because it's beaten into your head from the time you can walk: no black soles on the basketball court! You'd think the state of Wisconsin would just ban black-soled shoes altogether, but then I guess folks would smuggle them across the border and that would be an even bigger mess. But it was nice to see Ashley's parents and her little brother, and Dad shaking hands with Coach K as they slapped each other's shoulders.

Oh, it was great. I could play like this for the rest of my life. Meaning: it was great to beat Hawley, but it was also great to feel so good at it. And confident enough to work with Kayla on our special plays, and team my brain up with Kari's mouth. Maybe Kari could go to St. Margaret's with me. Or I could just go wherever she did and be her point guard buddy for three years. Maybe.

We went out to Taco Bell afterward, Kari and me with Beaner and Tyler Dietz after their game. The place was really crowded and we stood in line for a long time, Beaner behind me making goofy little pigtails out of my hair and singing this song about how he was a bag of groceries. When we got up to the counter, he looked at the girl apologetically:

"No habla inglés."

"What?" asked the girl, totally clueless.

"I" — only he pronounced it *khhi,* really far back in his throat — "I speak no Engleesh. Frijoles, per favor, señorita. Señorita *linda.*" He smiled helplessly and pointed at the menu.

"What's he saying?" the girl asked.

Kari leaned forward. "Beans. For . . . mes . . . amigos."

The folks around us were cracking up. The girl sighed. "Can one of you please order?"

"I will," I said. Beaner looked disappointed, but I can't manage an accent even if I had any idea what to say. So I did the best I could with the other three pantomiming, Beaner shouting, "Olé!" whenever the girl put another item on our tray, and he gave her a big "Muchos gracias, señorita" when we paid.

We piled in to a table, Beaner taking all the straws to make a mustache. "I am . . . El Hombre," he announced, "I am . . . El Hombre Macho!"

Tyler had his arm around Kari; they were making out a little, to tell the truth.

"Hey! Enough with the smoochering, mes chicos!" Beaner ordered. "El Hombre no like the smoochering." He wiggled his straw mustache at me. "Is correct, señorita?"

It was a little embarrassing, but I didn't feel nearly as stressed as the last time we were here. Maybe I was getting used to being in the forefront of things. Getting used to the attention.

Kind of like the Hawley game, now that I thought about it. It had been rough, sure, but it hadn't been out of control. Once I got to college, to St. Margaret's or Ibsen even, the basketball would be just like that, the same amount of stress. Maybe less, even, but certainly not *more*. So really . . . Wow, I had just experienced the worst hoops pressure I'd ever face in my life! And I'd been fine! Just like I was fine with Beaner.

I laughed. "Is totally correct, señor."

Beaner put his arm around my shoulders. "You is no so good at the español, señorita."

I laughed even more, really grooving on that feeling of him next to me.

Then I glanced around.

Why, I dunno. Maybe it was . . . I don't know what it was. I just know I did it.

There, on the other side of Taco Bell, was Brian. Sitting at a table full of Hawley guys, all of them watching us. The guy next to Brian was holding his straw under *his* nose, clearly imitating Beaner, with a really snotty expression on his face.

Brian saw me . . . and you know what? He didn't look away.

That's what I'd expected him to do. What I'd bet money he'd do. Look away first thing. Race out the door. Dive through the window.

Instead, though, he just nodded. Gave me that little tip folks give each other across a room.

His buddy, the snotty one, said something, and Brian turned to him. I couldn't make out what Brian said, but the guy put the straw down really fast, the way little kids do when their parents say something sharp.

"You is no loving me?" Beaner asked over my shoulder.

I spun back to face our table. "I, um, is loving you much."

"Non non non! Is 'loving me mucho,'" corrected Beaner. "You smoochering me maybe, maybe later?"

I laughed extra loud, and squeezed closer, getting my shoulder doing that puzzle-piece thing against his. And I focused extra hard on what he was saying, and Kari and Tyler too, making sure with every fiber of my muscles that I didn't look around again.

And then, five minutes later maybe, I finally did. Brian and his buddies were putting their jackets on, chatting among themselves. He glanced over our way and shot me a big grin, one of those thousand-dollar smiles he's so good at, and then he left. Not running or anything. Just ambling out the door.

Kari was asking me something.

"What?" I said, because I'd totally missed it.

"You're really serious about St. Margaret's?"

There was this little pause. Just a second when it occurred to me that maybe things with Brian could still work out. Maybe he really had changed. Maybe seeing me with other people, with other guys, hearing from his father that I was dating, maybe it showed him I wasn't so embarrassing after all.

But then, just as fast, I realized I was being stupid. Me going out with Brian wasn't any different from me playing D-I. Those were two leagues, D-I and Brian, that simply were not safe. Not for me, anyway. I'd just end up getting hurt. Getting hurt *again*. And hurting a lot of other folks when it came to basketball, coaches and players and fans and my family most of all. It wasn't fair to me or anyone else to set myself up for all that pain.

"D.J.?" Kari asked, kind of tugging me back down to Earth.

I dug in to my burrito. "Am I serious about St. Margaret's? One hundred percent. Absolutely."

9
HO HO OOPS

DAD FINALLY DID IT. He bit the bullet and decided to leave his cows and go see Win. Mom's begging paid off, hers and the Otts', and Dad's new BFF Mr. Nelson. Dad has left the farm overnight before, of course, but the way he carries on you'd think he was married to each and every one of his milkers. Mom and Win were coming home for Christmas, though, for two nights, so it made extra sense for him to learn about taking care of Win and then help them drive home.

Even so, I still didn't have the energy to drag that Christmas stuff out of the attic, and it looked like Dad and Curtis didn't either. Instead we spent the day before Dad left watching college hoops. Then that evening Amber and Dale came over to make popcorn balls because apparently that's a big tradition in Dale's family, and she and Dad talked barbecue together — Dale would be Dad's new BFF if Mr. Nelson wasn't — and she promised again to make Dad a smokehouse so he could make his own smoked cheese, both of them acting like this would actually happen and the rest of us going along with it.

The popcorn recipe says you have to boil this sugar water until it's really sticky, which Dale did, and then everyone works really fast to make the balls before the syrup cools too much. Only something went wrong somewhere, good old Schwenk luck, because we all ended up covered — I mean *covered* — in popcorn. It was stuck to Curtis's shirt, my hair, all over Smut, which she of course loved; it was like Christmas had come early for her. Oh, we were laughing. I don't think I've ever heard Dad laugh like that. We ended up with a couple of popcorn blobs with bits of lint and dirt, and some of Smut's fur, that Dad wrapped for Mom. Only he was laughing so hard that little tears were squeezing out of his eyes all over the wax paper, and the rest of us were laughing too hard to help. Every once in a while someone would act out opening one of those hairy blobs and we'd collapse all over again.

Sunday morning Dad took off finally, and Curtis and I immediately went back to sleep. Only just as I fell into bed there was a big pounding at the door, and before I could get there to open it all these ladies wearing Santa hats piled in.

"Ho ho ho!" called Kathy Ott. "Ho ho ho!"

"Merry Christmas!" other ladies hollered, marching in with boxes and cookie tins and a real live Christmas tree. Curtis took one peek and bolted back to his room. That guy would be a lot happier in the long run if he learned to sleep in sweatpants.

"It seemed like you needed a little help," Kathy explained. "I hope you don't mind."

"Oh no, this is great —"

Another lady stopped in front of me, a box on her hip: "Hello, D.J. I'm Betsy Nelson." She put out her hand. "Brian's mother." She was really pretty, which I guess I should have expected, and not heavy in the way a lot of moms around here get, which I should have expected just as much. "I baked some decorations for the tree," she said with a smile.

"Oh. That's nice." Then my brain started working a little, finally. "For the tree?"

She laughed, a really nice laugh. "That was the idea."

I eyeballed Smut, who at the moment was pretty spooked, but still sniffing for food because that's her natural condition. Checking the air just in case. "I don't think they'll last too long there."

"Ah. Excellent point," she said. "Why don't I just leave this somewhere and you can do it later?"

And that's how the afternoon went, the ladies all so helpful and flexible, with all these spruce branches and paper snowflakes, things we wouldn't even have to pack up when Christmas was over, which was just so amazingly thoughtful of them.

At one point I ended up next to Mrs. Nelson, after I'd made coffee, which everyone said they didn't need but took a cup of anyway, and a couple ladies unpacked food just in case anyone was on the brink of starvation right at that moment, which might explain why some ladies around here end up looking the way they do. "I'm so glad to finally meet you," she said, sounding just like the Oprah-talk-therapy lady she is.

I nodded. It was pretty weird to think about this lady being Brian's mother — even weirder than Mr. Nelson as his dad. I knew a lot about her, really: How she and Mr. Nelson didn't get along. How they were even talking about splitting up once Brian was gone. My ears turned red, remembering that stuff in front of her.

She came a bit closer. "I want to thank you for everything you've done for Brian."

"Oh. Sure." I wondered what he'd told her. Especially about our last fantastic conversation, right here in this very kitchen. Did he tell her he thought he'd been a jerk? That I'd cried, or almost cried, right in front of him? That —

"He had some maturing to do, you know . . ." She gave my arm a squeeze. "If you need anything, just give me a shout. Anything at all."

I need your son, I wanted to say. But that was just stupid. Besides, he'd walked away from me — walked away three times, when I thought about it. Last fall, and then in the kitchen, and then again Friday night at Taco Bell. So I didn't *need* Brian at all, thank you. I didn't need that suffering. Instead I poured everyone more coffee and ate some walnut bars Dad was going to have to get the recipe for, and took a call from Beaner asking me out.

Which was pretty cool, actually, talking to Beaner with Mrs. Nelson in the room possibly listening. Which I *should not be thinking,* darn it. I tried to focus on what Beaner was saying, although it was hard because he was talking so fast, something about Christmas and singing and his sister — Abby wanted me to come over, which was sweet, that I had a date with both of them. He even offered to pick me up. And then the ladies finished up, so thrilled to help out . . .

I swear, every person I know gets far more satisfaction from doing good deeds than receiving them. Maybe that's the whole point in the end, all of us putting up with good deeds, tolerating them as best we can, counting the minutes until we have the opportunity to reciprocate.

Curtis wasn't around for all this excitement because he'd gone off Christmas shopping with Sarah, which all the decorating ladies had found adorable, and I'd saved some of their "Isn't he cute" lines for later. So it was just me in the barn for evening milking. It was okay, though. I still had plenty of time to get ready for Beaner. The barn was nice and toasty from all those warm cow bodies, the windows covered in frost, and I was actually singing Christmas carols. Then I heard Sarah's mother pulling in to drop off Curtis, which was nice too, because now he and I could kid around and sing carols together.

I was on "The Twelve Days of Christmas," which is my favorite, and bungling the order which I always do, although just my singing would bungle it because carrying a tune isn't what we Schwenks do best, when Curtis walked in.

Only it wasn't Curtis.

For the second time in two weeks, I'd been blindsided by Brian Nelson.

Only this was even worse than in the kitchen, because I was so surprised to see him that I fell off my milking stool. And then Bennie Cunningham flicked her tail in my face, hard, to let me know how she felt about my behavior.

Brian tried really hard, you could tell, but he couldn't help cracking up, especially because Bennie wouldn't let up and I had to grab her tail before she flicked out my eyeball.

"You're supposed to warn people before you walk up on them singing," I said, doing my best to sound both angry and laid back.

"Yeah, I can see why." He grinned at me.

I started hooking up Pat O'Dea. *What the heck was Brian Nelson doing in our barn?*

He nodded at Pat. "He's on a plaque at the University of Wisconsin, their Wall of Fame. You know he punted a hundred and ten yards once?"

"They said he did. But it was in a snowstorm so I'm not sure how much anyone could see."

"Yeah . . . It was pretty cool, though, knowing his name. Being able to say I'd heard of him."

"Did you mention you'd learned it from a cow?" Because of course Dad names all his cows after football players — some pretty obscure ones sometimes. I mean, obscure now. I'm sure Pat O'Dea was famous back in 1899.

"Oh, yeah, absolutely. I was like, 'I milk cows all the time' . . . So, want me to start prepping?"

All of a sudden I remembered Mr. Nelson, his conversation with Dad about sending Brian over. "Is that why you're here? To help out?"

"Yeah. My old man really likes the idea of me going to the aid of a lady."

Which was so rich that I had to throw a rag at him.

"Thank you," he said, like I'd given him candy. "By the way, I hear you played a smoking game Friday night."

"Oh. Yeah. Hey, who's number twenty-three, anyway? Friend of yours?"

"Who? Oh, I know who you're talking about." He snorted. "She pushed me off the monkey bars once."

Which led to a discussion of *that*, Brian making me laugh over all the ways girls used to beat him up — because they liked him, which even I knew. That's how grade school girls show they like you, and middle school girls too sometimes, which I had to tease him about. And he filled me in on colleges, how he was seriously looking at UW–Milwaukee and how cool Milwaukee was, as cool as Madison even. I told him about my calls to coaches, Brian laughing so hard that he spooked the cows.

"Come on! It wasn't that bad!"

I shook my head. "You have no idea. I thought I was going to hyperventilate."

"You know, every school that sends you a letter should include a paper bag, like they do on planes. 'In case D.J. has to talk.' " Then he ducked to avoid any rags headed his way.

We were just finishing, shoveling out the last of the muck, when another car pulled in, finally. Typical Curtis, missing all the work. Only once the engine stopped, I could hear "Oh-ooo, darling!" and my heart stopped. Because only one person I know sings like that, and it ain't my little brother.

"Whoa," Brian said. "I never thought of Curtis as a Beatles fan."

"It's not —" I started, and then Beaner came bounding in.

"Please belieeeve —" He saw Brian.

"Hey, Beaner," I said. "This is Brian Nelson. A friend of mine — um, ours . . ."

"Yo." Beaner nodded with that too-cool-to-smile thing guys do when they're too cool to smile.

Brian nodded back, just as cool. "Heard you guys played a good game Friday."

"Not good enough," Beaner said coldly. Because the Red Bend boys had lost.

This could not be happening to me. This is the kind of thing that happens on TV, on bad TV, where the girl's old boyfriend and her new boyfriend meet and say awkward things to each other while the girl flutters around and pretends nothing happened. Which, by the way, nothing had. Brian was here because his dad made him. It's not like we were fooling around or anything, like it's so naughty to throw rags at each other. But what was I supposed to say? I'd only make it worse, because trying to make something sound innocent always backfires — I know that just from being a kid. And — and this is totally getting to the heart of the matter — if it *was* so innocent, then why did I feel so darn guilty?

So the silence lasted about ten years, and then Brian asked, because he's obviously much better at this sort of thing than I am, "You need any more help?"

"I think I've got it," I said. "But, um, thanks."

"You worked here over the summer," Beaner said to Brian. Didn't ask: said.

"Feels like old times, only colder." Which should have made us laugh but didn't.

I remembered one thing at least as Brian headed for the door. "Hey, could you thank your mom for this afternoon? That was really nice of her. Of all of them."

"Sure." Brian grinned. "But I wouldn't eat those cookies if I were you." Then he nodded at Beaner and he was gone.

Another itchy silence.

"Does he help out a lot?" Beaner asked, finally.

"Nah. My dad's picking up Win, so his father sent him over. You know, to 'help a lady.' " Which we also should have laughed at. But we didn't.

It was all back to normal, though, by the time I came down after a fifteen-second shower to find Beaner shooting the breeze with Kathy Ott, who was staying with us while Dad was gone. Curtis and I had said over and over that she didn't need to, that we didn't need babysitters for crying out loud, but Mom had seen this TV program about teenagers and the house-wrecking parties they threw and she wouldn't budge. I even pointed out that we don't know enough kids to throw a party and also that our house is already wrecked, but strangely enough that didn't help.

Beaner was cracking Kathy up as he finished off the walnut bars, telling her how we had to go back to his house to test out Abby's Christmas present. Which Abby was so excited about that she'd talked her folks into letting her open it early. And Beaner was so excited — well, half excited and half joking-excited — that he'd invited me and the Jorgensen twins and their boyfriend and girlfriend over so we all could test it out together. Because what Abby had wanted more than anything in the world was a karaoke machine.

Okay. If you had to guess my twenty-five favorite things in life, you probably wouldn't include karaoke. If you had to guess the top twenty-five hundred. But it was okay, once we got to Beaner's and he and Abby started, and were acting so goofy that no one could possibly be self-conscious about their own performance. Abby's friend Gabby was there too, of course, and the two of them did this song about feeling like a natural woman, with Abby singing and Gabby doing backup. They'd been practicing for weeks apparently. Then the three of them, Abby and Gabby and Beaner, acted out a song about twisting and shouting that apparently the three of them had been working on — that's how great a brother Beaner is — and it was so funny that Kyle Jorgensen's girlfriend had to scuttle to the bathroom like a crab so she wouldn't wet her pants.

We all performed, even me, though I made them pick out a Christmas carol because those are the only songs I know, and for once in my life I sang "The Twelve Days of Christmas" the right way because I could follow along with the words. Everyone joined in on the "five golden rings" bit, really drawing it out so we had to rush through all the little birds before the verse ended. And Beaner's mom made popcorn that wasn't sticky-furry, and we drank tons of pop, and we ended up having a huge snowball fight in their yard with their dog going crazy trying to dig up every snowball, so confused about why the ball had landed but now there wasn't anything there but snow. I could have spent a couple hours tossing snowballs to that screwy dog, it was so hilarious.

Beaner drove me home, singing about how it was the end of the world but he felt fine, drumming on my leg. We kissed good night, a long kiss, and I didn't even have to slow him down or anything seeing as Kathy was right there in the kitchen.

"Merry Christmas," he said.

I tweaked his Santa hat. He looked so cute in a Santa hat. "Merry Christmas to you too."

When I got inside Kathy wanted to hear all about the karaoke machine, laughing and laughing as I described it. I even acted out some of the dance moves myself, I was so loosened up. She said it sounded like a ton of fun.

It *had* been a ton of fun, I decided as I lay in bed that night. But if it was so fun, why all of a sudden did I feel so sad?

Because, I realized, figuring it out at last, as great as the singing and goofing off and popcorn and snowballs had been, and the kissing, I would have traded it all, without a single speck of regret, for five more minutes of mucking out the barn with Brian.

10
SAME OLD NEW YEAR

BILL DIDN'T MAKE IT HOME until Monday morning. He and Aaron pulled in around eleven while Kathy and I were sitting at the kitchen table, Kathy writing Christmas cards because I guess Schwenks aren't the only ones who leave things until the last minute, and me making presents. As soon as we caught sight of them, though, I was out the door — barefoot, so you can imagine — to give Bill an enormous hug, and almost as enormous a hug to Aaron, who's so big that he really needs two hugs just to get around him all the way.

Right away they took me out Christmas shopping. Which meant I got to ride shotgun next to Aaron as the two of them busted each other and listed all the reasons I should go to the U of M.

"Plus you'd be an itty-bitty freshman when we're seniors," Aaron pointed out. Which, you know, had already occurred to me. It gave me a pang, I have to say, the thought of how great it'd be to have these big handsome guys on campus showing me the ropes. Or how great it *would* have been, seeing as now I wasn't going there. I didn't say anything, though, because then they would have gone off on how I actually *am* D-I material, and besides, what do they even know about disappointing people? They deal with pressure like that all the time. So I just kept my mouth shut and nodded, and giggled whenever they called each other Milkshake and Tink. Although I didn't have the guts to call Aaron Tink because I'm not, you know, on the University of Minnesota football team. And I didn't call Bill Milkshake because I don't want to die.

We went to the local mall — which Aaron couldn't help pointing out was teeny compared to the malls *he* knew — and because Bill and I have about eighteen cents between us, we bought socks and potholders and pencils, things everyone always needs (well, Dad needs potholders) that don't cost very much. Aaron kept finding stuff like cheesehead hats that I guess you only see in Wisconsin, and he was having a blast. By the time we finished it was already time for afternoon milking, which Aaron quote-unquote helped with, which meant making Bill and me laugh our guts out while *we* did the actual work. The cows just flicked their ears like they'd heard all his jokes before. Once I couldn't help myself and squirted Aaron with milk, and Mark Donahue kicked me to teach me a lesson about fooling around with her own personal mammary glands.

Aaron spent the night in the little office before driving home to Detroit, making me promise to wake him when I got up for morning milking, which I did even though his bellyaching makes Brian Nelson sound positively saintly. But we still got him off before dawn, with a couple huge thermoses of coffee because he had one long drive ahead of him, all the way past Chicago. Then we ran around like crazy getting ready — you always think everything's ready and it always turns out not to be so — for Win's arrival, including shoveling the parking space again and sweeping off Mr. Nelson's nice new ramp and decorating it with a couple big bows.

Win's arrival — oh, boy. He could wheel himself out of the van, and up the ramp, and get from his chair to his bed without barely any help at all, and use a fork and everything. He was a lot thinner, but that's probably better for anyone who has to lift him. He was really psyched about the ramp too, and told Dad he'd done a really fantastic job, which cracked everyone up and made Dad a bit huffy. Mom of course said that Dad could have built the ramp if he'd wanted, which is a stretch coming from her seeing as she's lived with his carpentry skills for twenty-five years. And she was thrilled to bits about the decorating.

Guess what we did Christmas Eve? Not caroling or opening gifts or giving food to folks poorer than us. We watched Mr. Jorgensen's tape of the Hawley game. Seriously. Win insisted, and he parked himself in front of our TV with the remote because he said it was therapy, when really holding the remote is just his old controlling self. Mom wanted to watch too, and Bill since they hadn't seen it, so we all ended up in the living room, me sitting in the back wincing. Win kept pausing to point stuff out, letting me know how far I was from perfect. And he hit the roof about that bad call on Kari, so it's good he hadn't been at the game or Ashley would have had two guys to baby-sit. But afterward he said that he needed a couple copies of the tape, so I guess I wasn't so far from perfect. And I made a mental note to get copies to St. Margaret's and Ibsen most of all.

Win especially liked how Ashley had calmed Coach K down. He said that was exactly the kind of leadership he was talking about, my directing her like that, and that I should be doing that sort of thing all the time. I couldn't help thinking it was just the opposite, that college coaches would be disgusted to see me bossing around adults, and besides, I'd only been trying to keep Coach K from embarrassing us. It had nothing to do with leadership at all. And then Mom said it was bedtime and if we didn't hurry Santa wouldn't come. Which made us laugh, but we still hurried off to bed anyway.

Christmas morning I got up to milk — that was part of my gift to Dad — but it turned out he was up already, so the two of us did it together. You see, for Christmas I made him two Get Out of Milking Free cards, like those Get Out of Jail ones. There was joking about that, you can be sure, later that morning when we opened presents, and even more about two certificates I gave Win that promised I Will Listen To Your Advice, and way down at the bottom in tiny letters the words As Much As I Can. Even Win had to laugh at that. And there were the socks and pencils and potholders, and stuff Win made in art therapy that wouldn't have looked any better if he had functional hands because Schwenks and art simply don't mix. And Mom had knitted everyone hats that were kind of scratchy but still awfully nice and colorful. And Dad made everyone peanut brittle that left us all speechless because we couldn't unlock our jaws. And his Christmas dinner was extra delicious, and as we sat down with Bill still wearing his scratchy hat, Mom said how nice it was to all be a family again. So all in all it was a fantastic Christmas even with only our eighteen cents.

The next day Mom and Dad and Win left for the hospital, Dad to help drive and also because he'd kept his pickup there, and Bill and I went over to the high school. Win had made me get keys to the gym because heaven forbid I wouldn't practice practice practice and then report to him what I'd done. We played one on one and horse, messing around and goofing on each other. Bill told me about a girl he was seeing who he was actually kind of serious about, which is a big first for him, and I filled him in a bit on Beaner and how crazy he is. Bill loved hearing about the pep rally, and he made me act the whole thing out and walk the way Beaner had walked and everything. He said Beaner sounded even funnier than he used to be, when he was just a skinny freshman Bill's senior year, and that he must be a pretty great guy. Which wasn't the worst thing in the world to hear.

So it was pretty awesome when Beaner agreed — not that I had to twist his arm, but apparently he had all these relatives he was supposed to, you know, *entertain,* so he didn't have a lot of free time — but the next day he got away somehow and joined us. We talked Curtis into coming too, and then the four of us played until we could barely move. Bill's so big and so fast from football that his side always had a huge advantage, although Beaner's taller even than Bill and really fights for every rebound, and it's not like I'm some sort of wallflower. And Curtis, well, don't ever underestimate him. In hoops and also, you know, in life. Because while we were goofing off and laughing, taking these extremely illegal and hilarious shots, Curtis just kept plugging away, basket after basket, making the three of us look pretty darn lame.

Then when we were stopped for a water break after a couple hours of this (we'd forgotten ice like a bunch of idiots, but luckily there was fresh snow right outside!) Beaner said to Bill, "Hey, I'm throwing this New Year's Eve party, you know, if you're around. You too, Curtis."

Curtis immediately looked like he'd rather die, but Bill perked right up because there's nothing he likes like a party. Beaner described how his mom and stepdad were paying him back for entertaining all those lame relatives from Sheboygan, and how he was going to get Abby's karaoke machine going, and kids could even sleep over if they wanted . . .

I sat there for like ten minutes listening to Beaner and Bill plan this out, Bill tossing in suggestions on how to make the party better and saying how totally bummed he was about missing it because he loved karaoke (Hello? Are we even related?), while I got more and more miserable because here was Beaner inviting my brothers, who he barely even knows, and he hadn't even invited *me*. His *girlfriend*. I guess he didn't want me there. This was just his Beaner way of telling me that. Maybe he wasn't that different from Brian after all.

So I said, trying as hard as I could to seem nonchalant, "Well, it sure sounds like fun."

"Oh, it'll be awesome —" Beaner said, and then he looked at me with this expression of absolute horror and said, "Holy crap, I forgot to invite you."

Well, Bill just about fell off the bleachers laughing at *that*. Even Curtis broke up. Especially because Beaner spent another ten minutes explaining he assumed I knew I was invited, and what a jerk he was, and how just to pay him back I could make him sing any song I wanted, even that song where that girl who's a really good singer keeps saying she's not going.

Then of course he went out onto the court and sang it, right then and there, and Bill literally — I am not exaggerating — had to lie down so that he wouldn't keel over. I have to say that it was a pretty impressive way for Beaner to apologize, especially at the end, when he dropped to one knee and swung his arms around and everything.

Later, after we'd gone home, Curtis and me having to listen to Bill crack up every time he thought about Beaner, I called Mom to ask her permission and right away she said *You are not sleeping over* in that tone that means don't even think about arguing. That woman was watching too much television, the way she carried on like teenagers are all pregnant juvenile-delinquent idiots. But at least she said I could go to Beaner's for a little while.

Before any of that happened, though, I needed to visit the University of Wisconsin–Madison, even though the school was on break, because Win wanted me to see this hoops tournament they were holding.

Which is really something to think about, in and of itself. I mean, most college students cut classes whenever they feel like it and stay out late, basically get to do anything they want. But not athletes. Athletes have curfews every night, and hours of workouts every single day, not just practice but weights and flexibility and meetings, and they have to play in every single game, show up even if they're injured or benched or something, because that's their scholarship requirement. And travel all over the country, getting back to their dorms at two or three in the morning maybe, but even so, they can't skip class. Or they miss a whole week of classes because of tournaments and have to run around afterward getting all caught up. And even when everyone else is off enjoying winter break, and spring break too, when that happens, they're still at school playing. Bill had to leave Saturday morning, just as I was driving off to Madison, for this camp thing he'd signed up for. He'd only had five days of vacation, after a whole semester packed with football and classes and papers and exams.

Thinking about that, I was doubly relieved with my secret no D-I decision. Because even though I wanted to get out of Red Bend ASAP, I'd like to come back occasionally. Come back for more than "Hello, thanks for the scratchy hat, I've got a game two thousand miles away." That was one great thing about St. Margaret's and Ibsen: at least they take a breather every once in a while. They don't have round-the-clock athlete curfews. That was nice to know.

So I drove to Madison all by myself, which the UW people sounded a little weird about because I guess you're supposed to show up with your folks seeing as college is such a Big Decision. But of course Mom and Dad couldn't come, and Kathy Ott had already done enough for us. Too much, really. And I kept insisting I was totally okay, and I promised Mom I'd be extra safe and would stop driving the second it started to snow.

It must sound pretty strange that I was going to all this effort, driving ten hours just to keep Win off my back. But the real reason I was going — not that I would ever tell this to anyone, not in a million years — was that I needed a haircut. Seriously. I was about ready to duct-tape my hair back, it was driving me so crazy. I hadn't had it cut since the summer, when Curtis and I had driven to Madison and I'd found this really cool salon with this really cool girl named Mica who gave me this totally awesome haircut because she was so psyched I was trying out for football. I even saved the little card she'd given me, even though at the time I knew I'd never, ever be back. But guess what, now I was, and I'd even snuck into our downstairs bathroom where no one could hear me and made an appointment.

So I was pretty psyched to be hitting the road, and I spent most of the drive imagining how I'd explain to Mica that I'd quit football, hoping she wouldn't be too disappointed in me. But wouldn't you know it, she already knew. And taped to her mirror was that *People* article! And a little sticky note next to it saying I CUT HER HAIR!!!

Well, that was something to see. And I guess it shows that everyone's different. I mean, there I was so impressed with Mica and her cool salon, so intimidated, and at the same time Mica was just as impressed with this cheesehead hick that was me. Isn't that funny?

She didn't even act disappointed about my having to quit. She said she understood completely, and once she found out I was back in town to look at UW, she just went off on how cool Madison is, making it sound like her city was the only place in the world to play basketball or study or live or basically to breathe. I didn't point out that people breathe in other cities too, and even in the countryside sometimes, because she was so sparkly and excited. But I did decide that wherever I ended up, that school had to play in Madison once or twice a year, so I'd be able to keep looking halfway okay. It's too bad when you find a decent haircut you can't just freeze it there and not unfreeze it until you're sure you can make it back to Madison.

Just so you know, the Badgers arena is *huge*. Bigger even than the U of M's, and all set up for TV broadcasts. Only most of the seats were empty when I showed up, because I guess a women's tournament in the middle of winter break doesn't attract too much attention. Even so, walking in I got that same icy feeling in my stomach, seeing all those empty seats and knowing that sometimes they were full of people all ready to judge whoever it was out there on the floor, and I was doubly, triply relieved that whoever that person was wouldn't be me.

I met the assistant coach who'd been talking to Win, who of course said how excited he'd be to have me in their program, what a hard worker I was and how much Coach K respected me, and who talked my ear off as he showed me around. And I knew enough to bounce his compliments right back at him, telling him how great the arena was, and his team. Plus I answered all his questions about Win and the work the two of us had done together, which he really wanted to hear about.

One of the players showed me around campus that night, telling me *again* how utterly fantastic Madison is, and when she heard I'd seen their game against the U of M, she got all pumped. I didn't have the heart to tell her that the girl who'd lost was kind of my friend. Because it wasn't her fault that Tyrona missed two free throws, or that I almost threw up.

I was as nice as I could be — I guess *tactful* is how you'd describe it — agreeing with them all the time, but also saying I was looking at other schools and Madison was five hours from home, and tough academically for someone with my little brain. I didn't put it quite like that, but I made the point. Got across that they should be looking at other players as well, at lots of them.

Driving back, that super-long five-hour drive, I couldn't help thinking about Brian. I'd controlled myself for a good long while there, but then it snuck in when my guard was down, just as I was stopping for gas. I went in to get myself a pop and saw the milk cartons all lined up in the case and *pow*, there went all my protection. Dang, it had been nice milking with him! Even seeing him in Taco Bell had been nice. He'd been so different that night, in the two seconds we'd actually looked at each other. Maybe he really had done some of that growing up that his mom and Tyrona mentioned. People do change, you know; they change all the time. Look how much easier my dad is to deal with just since this summer. If Dad can change, well, anyone can. You know, if I went to Madison and Brian went to Milwaukee, we'd be less than two hours apart. We could visit on weekends, and maybe he could even come to my games . . .

I slapped myself across the face — really hard. So hard it left a huge mark on my cheek, but I had to do it. I was driving again when I did this, so at least I didn't freak anyone at the gas station out. But I had to show myself just how *stupid* I was. For one thing, I was not going to Madison, for reasons I believe I've explained in pretty thorough detail. And even if I did go there, because I'd lost my mind or something, having Brian watch me play would be pretty much the stupidest thing ever. The thought of playing in front of strangers makes me freeze up; imagine how well I'd do in front of him. They'd have to take me off the court on a stretcher. Besides which — besides the fact that I wasn't ever going to play D-I ball — there was also, thank you, another guy in my life. Who didn't give me goose bumps, sure, but at least he never made me cry. Which is a big huge check in the plus column. And who loved going out with me — I mean, literally "going out," as in movies and hoops games and Taco Bell. And who could make me laugh — laugh so hard I could barely stand up sometimes. Which is also a big huge check.

Just thinking about that karaoke night at Beaner's made me smile. Sure, I'd gotten all soppy later about Brian, but you can't deny that I'd had a blast, tossing snowballs to the Halstaads' dog and busting a rib at the sight of everyone twisting and shouting away. Plus Beaner was throwing a New Year's Eve party — the first one I'd ever gone to that was just for kids instead of a family party with my parents and stuff. With kids *sleeping over*, even. *Plus* thanks to my new haircut I was actually going to look okay. Which was nice to think about too, and got me singing about twisting and shouting the rest of the way home.

I wore a skirt for once, which was good because the other girls were really dressed up, Kari in this slinky dress that looked amazing, and Beaner's basement had streamers and glittery mirror balls and colored light bulbs. Amber and Dale were in St. Paul visiting friends of Dale's — not that they would have gone to Beaner's, but they didn't even have the chance to say no, which I have to say was kind of a relief, not having to worry about them — but there were tons of hoops players there. And some punch that I knew better than to taste, having seen Bill get sick on punch once. That's an image that stays with you awhile, that one. Plus, Abby and Gabby hung around acting like they were teenagers too. Which they almost were, those girls are so mature.

The girls were extra excited to see me, and made me come up to Abby's room so they could play with my hair, telling me how great my new haircut was, and wouldn't you know, it actually looked better when they were done. And they insisted I wear lip gloss, which Abby had a suitcase of it looked like, and they wanted to put big glittery earrings on me but I was happy just with the studs that were in there, the same studs I've had since I got them pierced because really I don't need anything else.

After a while the karaoke started, and Abby and Gabby did their dance routine until Beaner finally got his mom to drag them upstairs. Then the punch got everyone going, I guess, or maybe Beaner's natural unembarrassedness relaxed them. A couple guys performed a song about "gimme some loving" — that's the only line I could make out — and they were really good, although Kari whispered that they were just copying the Blues Brothers, which made me really want to see that movie if it could get two Red Bend basketball players dancing like that. Kari sang too, spelling out the word *respect* and dancing around in her dress like, well, like a girl who really knows how to dance. Her boyfriend looked surprised even.

After Kari was done singing, the two of them got a little hot and heavy in the corner. And it gave me a pang. Maybe it was because I wasn't drinking, I don't know. Every once in a while Beaner would give me a hug, just being friendly, and that was great. He even got me dancing which normally only Aaron does and only when I'm outside Wisconsin. But even so, I was getting that feeling like I didn't belong there anymore. Plus Mom had given me this huge lecture about all the drunk drivers out on New Year's Eve and she'd be a lot happier once she knew I was home.

So I said goodbye. Beaner wanted me to stay until midnight but I said I needed to get up for milking. Which wasn't a complete lie seeing as Dad still had time to call in his coupons, and it sounded better than saying I just felt out of place. Kari gave me a huge sloppy hug — she'd had a lot of punch, it looked like — and some boys slapped my hand, and I said good night to Beaner's mom, reassuring her I hadn't had anything stronger than pop, and finally I was outside in that cold cold air, just me and the stars so far away.

I started the Caravan and sat there while it warmed up, enjoying the quiet after all that noise. You know — you know what I really wanted? Brian.

Which was *stupid*. I know. I know that. But I felt this emptiness, like I was a mitten and he was the only mitten that matched. Which probably sounds like I really had been drinking, but I was sober. Crazy, sure, but sober.

So I called him. Which I shouldn't have done. But he'd helped with milking, which I'm sure he could have gotten out of if he'd really insisted, no matter what his dad might have said. And at Taco Bell he'd actually looked happy to see me, and had even told his friends off, it looked like, for being jerks. And he'd come to my house, that kitchen-visit day, just to apologize. And had saved me some coffee cake, just one more little way of showing he still wanted to be friends. So you know, maybe it was time for me to do something too. So it wasn't just him doing the reaching out.

That's why I called. To show that I could connect too. Leave a Happy New Year message on his cell. Just a message would be enough.

But instead he answered. To my total shock. Actually he hollered, over this incredibly loud music and screaming. "Hey! D.J.! How are ya?"

I held the phone away from my ear. "I'm great."

"What?"

"Great —"

"I can't hear you! Wait a sec!" A bunch of noise, and then silence. "Wow. It's really cold."

"You're *outside?*" I had to laugh.

"I'm in my car, actually. Hey — hey! Where are you?"

"I'm in New York City waiting for the ball to drop."

"Really? Oh, ha ha. Really, where are you?"

"I'm in Red Bend. Where are *you?*"

"I'm in Hawley . . . Hey, you know that gas station with the cow out front? Can you drive there?"

"Meaning do I know how to get there or can I drive?" The Caravan was warming up, finally. I could talk to Brian forever.

"Can you drive. Because I could meet you there."

"Aren't you at a party?" But I was already pulling out.

"It's totally lame. They wanted to play Spin the Bottle — can you believe it? Plus the closet they picked was all mildewy."

I laughed. "You're kidding."

"No way. I have this buddy with asthma — he's like, 'I'll play if you want but I have to bring my inhaler in with me.'"

"That's romantic. Bet the girls couldn't wait to kiss him."

"Yeah. Let's go make out with The Lung." He cracked up.

We talked the whole way to the gas station, me keeping watch for homicidal drunk drivers although there was almost no one on the road, which would be one good thing to report to Mom. When I pulled up Brian was already there, and he jumped out of his Cherokee and into the Caravan, rubbing his hands together.

"Hey," I said. Smiling at him.

"Hey. Here." He held out a little package with beat-up wrapping paper, trying to straighten the bow. "I meant to give it to you before but . . ."

"That's okay. You didn't have to get me anything!"

Brian shrugged. "I know. Go ahead, open it."

Inside all that beat-up wrapping paper was a box, and inside that box was tissue paper. And inside the tissue paper was a pair of little gold earrings stamped like basketballs.

"Oh, Brian . . ."

"They're not real gold. I mean, the stems are, that's what the lady said, but the rest is gold plate. Or they'd cost like thousands of dollars . . ."

"They're perfect. They're absolutely perfect."

And they looked perfect too, in my earlobes, because of

course I put them on right away. And my hair was now the perfect length to show them off.

"Thank you," I said. Thinking to myself that if this was a movie, it would be a really good time to kiss. If, you know, anyone in the Caravan happened to be leaning that way.

"You're welcome." He beamed at me. "I was really afraid I wouldn't be able to get them to you. They look fantastic with your hair, by the way. That's an awesome haircut."

"Thanks." Was it cheating to kiss someone who'd just given you earrings? But I didn't want to think that right at this moment; it was too girly and complicated and too not-now.

"Hey!" Brian said, glancing at the clock. "It's midnight."

I looked over. "No, it's not. It's eleven."

He leaned in closer. "Not in New York. Happy New Year."

The whole drive home, I was on a cloud. It's a good thing I didn't encounter any homicidal drunk drivers, because I probably would have crashed right into them. Now *that's* kissing, I kept thinking to myself, this little thing inside my head. Kind of like my free-throw chant but, well, not. Because you know, I hadn't just been imagining it. Brian really did know how to kiss. It was fireworks and rockets even without it being midnight.

I didn't think about Beaner — isn't that awful? Not once. Not until I was home. Because I had a sense I already knew the answer to my cheating question. Kissing ex-boyfriends is definitely a no-no. I didn't like the idea of doing a no-no, and I especially didn't like the idea of doing that to Beaner.

Which led to the next thought. The thought that sucked all the happiness right out of my body, every single little molecule. Beaner had invited me to his New Year's Eve party. Which turned out not to be my scene, but that wasn't his fault. And it was kind of cool that Brian left *his* party, wherever that was, just to hang out with me at a cheesy gas station. But didn't that just bring Brian and me right back to square one? Because Brian had always been good at that. At hanging out with me in private. Once again he'd left his real friends to slink away and see me on the side. And once again I'd let him.

11
D.J. Schwenk Is Not Magic Johnson

So you can imagine how nice New Year's Day was, for me and for anyone who wasn't smart enough to stay a couple of counties away. I finally went over to the gym and shot for hours, playing as hard as I could so I wouldn't have to think anymore.

That night I lay staring at my ceiling and wondering why I was such a total sucker, such a *loser* for falling for Brian yet again. Falling for a guy who was nothing more than a sneak. So what if Beaner couldn't kiss perfectly — at least he didn't act like I had cooties. He'd kiss me in front of the whole school without batting an eye. He'd look forward to it, even. Send out invitations . . . Not that I wanted that, really — ever — but still. Still.

Dad came clumping upstairs. "You hear me? Win wants to talk to you."

I hadn't even heard the phone ring. "I'm busy," I said.

Dad stood in the doorway. "He's on the phone right now."

"I'm busy," I said again, studying my ceiling like there'd be a test on it on Monday.

Dad watched me for a minute, then headed back down. I could hear him talking but I couldn't make out what he was saying, and I sure as heck didn't care.

Brian called my cell, but I didn't pick up. I couldn't — what would I say? What could I say that I hadn't said already? He left a message, though, saying he'd try me later.

Which was good, actually, if anything in this horrible situation could be good, because it gave me time to plan. So when he called again, the next day, I was ready.

"Hey," I said. But it wasn't a happy *hey*.

"Hey, it's so great you're there —"

"Listen," I said, in my most serious voice. "We cannot do this. We cannot talk."

"What's wrong with talking?"

I sighed. "You know. I have someone now."

"That tall guy?"

"Yes, that tall guy. And I like him, and he likes me, and you know it will never work between us." It killed me to say this. But it was the truth.

"It could —"

"Come on, Brian. We've been here before. Let's not have history repeat itself." Which I'd learned in history class, that line, and I liked it a lot.

"You really believe that?"

"Yeah. I do. So . . . goodbye."

There was a bit of a silence, and I hung up. Super gently,

but I'm not sure he could tell that. Then I lay there, going over the conversation again and again. *I like him, and he likes me:* that's how I'd described Beaner. And it was true, I did like him. But that was the problem. I didn't feel anything more. I never felt a click. But there were so many other great things about Beaner that maybe asking for a click was just asking for way too much.

At least practice started again, Coach K figuring that anyone not lucky enough to go to Florida could get something out of winter break.

Ashley looked really excited to see me. Right away she asked if we could talk and I said okay, trying to figure out how to explain that I'd only visited Madison because of Mica, and because I needed to keep Win off my back.

Only it turned out Ashley didn't care so much about haircuts. She hadn't even known I'd been to Madison, although she said maybe we could hang out together if we both ended up going there — as if there was a chance I would and a chance she wouldn't. We were shooting baskets together after everyone else had left, grooving on having a real gym for once, when all of sudden she blurted out, her eyes all bright, "I've got an idea." She sidled a little closer. "I read this article last week about how a lot of actors are really shy."

"Then why are they actors?" I couldn't help pointing out.

"That's just it! Even famous actors — when they're in public as themselves, they're totally shy. But when they're playing someone else, they can do anything!"

"Uh, okay . . ."

"Don't you see? That's how you can play! That's how you can do all that stuff Coach K keeps bugging you about. Just pretend you're someone else!"

I drove away, then spun and shot a three-pointer. It missed. "What, I'm supposed to pretend I'm Magic Johnson?"

"Who's he?"

How are you supposed to take advice on basketball from someone who doesn't know the best point guard in the history of the game? "Never mind," I said. And then, "I'll think about it."

"Will you? Will you really?"

"Sure. Now let's work on some passing." Because passing at least made sense, not like pretending to be someone else. How could I pretend to be someone else when I was already failing at being the person I already was?

Finally on Monday school started up again, all of us razzing Kayla because she *had* gone to Florida and came back so tan you could scream, and everything was back to normal. Only it wasn't back to *normal* normal, if there is such a thing, because all these Brian thoughts kept starting up whenever I least expected them, and because of Win. It wasn't like he said to himself, *It sounds like D.J.'s busy so I'll just back off.* No, he was still on the horn calling coaches and getting Mr. Jorgensen's videos and setting up campus visits. Whenever he called, I just said whatever I could in order to get off the phone, then passed him off to Dad.

Tuesday we played Cougar Lake, which apparently had gotten rid of its lice. I tried to do what Ashley suggested, I really did, pretending I was Magic Johnson. But I am not him, in so many ways, that it just scrambled my brain. Finally I bagged the whole thing and just focused on the game instead.

But you know what? I actually did okay. Not because I was Magic Johnson; maybe it was because I was so aware I wasn't Magic Johnson. I dunno. But I'd be thinking my automatic jock-type thoughts, like how Kari needed to guard 45 or Jess should double down on their best player with me, and then I'd remember with a jolt that Kari could help with this. And then I'd go find her to tell her to say something.

By the second half Kari and I were going downcourt together, talking away until she set herself up at the top of the key, organizing everyone else. And near the end of the game when I had some foul trouble, I even told everyone — all by myself with my very own mouth! — that I was switching to this Cougar Lake girl who was half my size and who stayed so far from the paint that I couldn't ever get accused of fouling *her*. So then their best player scored a couple times but at least I didn't foul out, which was awesome because I shot a three-pointer right at the end. Which we didn't need but it looked so sweet swishing through, nothing but net — it was like saving that one bit of pancake with all the butter on it for your very last bite. That's how nice it felt. So I guess you don't need to be Magic Johnson to win a game after all.

The next day Coach K went on and on about the leadership I'd demonstrated, how I'd called for double-teaming, how I pulled myself off when I'd gotten my fourth foul, acting like this was a big late Christmas present just for him. My ears went neon pink, I'm sure, watching everyone nod along with him. Then he brought up again, not even glancing my way, that any girl who was free after practice should hang around for my workouts with Ashley. And five girls including Kari and Brittany said okay, girls who also had to wait for their brothers and who apparently didn't want to spend that time on boring old homework.

It was pretty darn bizarre having them all there, let me tell you, and not only because of the look the cafeteria people gave us when we trooped in. It was bizarre how all the girls were looking at *me*. Like I was the coach or something. It's one thing to have little Ashley Erdel hang on everything I said, but this was different. Plus Kari and Brittany are both really good, which made it even harder.

But then I remembered Win. It'd be nice to able to tell him that for once I was doing something right. Then he'd talk my ear off about drills and techniques, how to review the basics because you can never get enough of the fundamentals, which is how Win actually talks. That would really make him happy, getting to jaw away like that, and maybe it would even get him to back off a little on all the other stuff he felt I should be doing.

So that's what we ended up focusing on, the fundamentals. Because Win is right for one thing, and I didn't want him chewing me out later. Besides, it's not my place to be designing plays or anything like that; lay-ups and passing and dribbling drills are more than enough.

And you know, it was really nice to discover I wasn't such a bad coach. I know I helped Brian last summer, and Ashley, who needs all the help she can get — she could get helped by anyone. But it was nice to see I could help other girls too, girls who were already pretty good. That I could come along and help them get a little bit better.

I even got to help Beaner — isn't that funny? Because the next day he talked his way out of the first couple minutes of *his* practice to hang out with us girls, which explains Beaner to a T. But he was being so puffy-rooster about it that I decided to take him down a notch or two, so we did this demonstration on stealing, and every time he stole the ball from me I'd steal it right back. I was trying to be educational, showing how you always have to protect your ball, but that point got lost in everyone's howling at how I was taking Beaner down. Of course then he started tickling, which got everyone howling even more, and I'll admit was pretty fun even for me.

Mr. Jorgensen even showed up a couple days after that to videotape us — not Beaner tickling, just a normal fundamentals practice. I guess the ice cream store business is so slow in January that he was pretty desperate for entertainment. And even that didn't faze me too much, because if Jerry Knudsen or the St. Margaret's coaches want to see me helping Ashley with her free throws or Brittany with her left-handed lay-ups, well, that probably wouldn't be so bad.

So maybe helping girls with their fundamentals was what did it. Maybe it was that I'd made peace with the kind of school I was going to — and maybe even the exact school I was going to, if everything worked out between me and St. Margaret's. Maybe it was Beaner's tickling and me trying to run away but not too much if you know what I mean. Whatever it was, our game Friday against Bison High turned out to be our best one yet. At least that's what Coach K said afterward, and I sure wasn't going to disagree.

The only bad thing was that late in the game Kari landed wrong and twisted her ankle. It wasn't that serious; she just sat icing it while hollering her lungs out from the bench. But it meant she'd be on crutches for a week or two, which was bad news for the team and was especially bad news for non–Magic Johnson D.J.

During the game I was too busy playing to think about what it would mean to lose my Kari Jorgensen vocal cords.

Over the weekend, though, the reality really sank in. Because it wasn't like I could rush over to our bench every time I had an idea and tell her what to shout to everyone; our system had been awkward enough as it was. And then Monday it got even worse, because it turned out that Kayla on Sunday bruised her tailbone playing pickup hockey. Which was exactly how she said it, "I bruised my tailbone," in this really tough voice to remind everyone not even to think of describing it any other way. She even had to carry a pillow everywhere to sit on.

This always happens, I know. Injuries are just part of basketball, you have to factor them in the same way you do bad foul shooting or a rebounder who always travels. Besides, it wasn't just our team that was suffering; that mean number 23 girl from Hawley tore her ACL playing Whoopsville and was going to need surgery, which shows why you shouldn't go around pinching people, because sooner or later you'll pay for it. But it was clear we were going to have make some changes, and Coach K spent most of Monday running through plays that drew out the clock instead of relying on a constant press like we were used to. He also started going pretty deep into the bench, so deep that he even had Ashley playing some, which meant even more work for me because I had to direct her in addition to everything else. A bunch of these girls hung around after practice, and we spent our cafeteria time reviewing K's new plays until even Ashley kind of understood them in her physics-brain way.

Beaner showed up too for a couple minutes, talking his way yet again out of his practice, and I couldn't help but interrupt our review work to play a little one-on-one, showing everyone how much better he was getting. Over the weekend he and I had used the gym for a couple hours both days, playing hard but goofing around too, like when he'd give me a kiss for a really good shot, or I'd put him in a bear hug to keep him down. Which we didn't do in front of all those girls, thank you very much, but the girls were pretty impressed with Beaner's improvement, applauding him and everything.

Our game Tuesday against New Norway was . . . Oh, man, I love playing full-court press. But it turns out that passing and passing and passing before each basket, taking as much time as you possibly can because your team doesn't have very strong players, well, it turns out that that can be really fun too, especially because New Norway got *so* frustrated waiting for us to do something, and sooner or later they let their guard down, every time, so that when we did shoot we usually scored. So, odd as it sounds, even though my points per game went down, my percentage went up. Isn't that funny?

Friday's game was just as wild. I still really missed Kari the human megaphone, but I have to say that this new playing style meant a lot less pressure on me. Plus West Lake isn't very good. So, again, it was one of the best games of the sea-

son, not because I scored a ton but because there wasn't any
of that frozen-stomach tension. It felt — not that I'll ever say
this to Coach K because he'd freak — but it felt like a driveway pickup game almost, only with a much better playing
surface and a bunch of kids we normally don't have over.
And no Smut getting underfoot breaking everyone's ankles,
which we certainly didn't need, not given the size of our
bench. Even Ashley scored. That's how great the game was.

So I was feeling pretty good about myself, on-court and
off-court as well. Now that the pain had faded a bit, I was
really proud of myself for taking the reins like that with
Brian, telling him it was over between us. Because it was. I
was so much better off with Beaner. Sure, he might embarrass me sometimes, and our romance wasn't exactly heart-
throbbing, but he was funny and supportive and an all-
around really great one-on-one guy.

The way my life was going, why, I couldn't imagine things
ever going south.

12
OPPORTUNITY STINKS

FIRST OF ALL, BEANER ASKED ME to the Valentine's Day dance. The Valentine's semiformal, actually. Not that I knew what a semiformal was except that I didn't have the clothes for it. That part I knew for sure.

Which would have been bad in and of itself — not him asking me really, but that I had to figure out the whole *clothing* business, which you might understand by now I'm not so good at, all that fashion girl stuff. But what made it eight billion times worse is that Beaner — you know how I just said he's great so long as I know to duck the embarrassing parts? Well, it turns out I'm not so good at anticipating when exactly those parts are going to be.

Because what happened was that after the West Lake game on Friday, I went out with Amber and Dale. Which I hadn't done in a while, what with all their traveling and my traveling and me hanging out with Beaner, and something called sleep, which I need every so often, not to mention school and homework . . . Anyway, I hadn't seen them for a really long time, and it really meant a lot to hang out and not talk college or recruiting or Magic Johnson and instead just have us *be*.

So there we were, the three of us, not even at Amber's because her mother was actually home for once, and instead we went out for pizza. The pizza place wasn't so great, and Dale and Amber couldn't help comparing it to Chicago, which apparently has a completely different species of pizza, it's so good, but it was a lot better than hanging out with Amber's mom. I didn't even care that my coat would smell like fried onions for a couple days, or that I'd have to take a shower afterward to get that smell out of my hair.

They were in the middle of describing this pizza place to me, the one in Chicago, trying to nail the accent of the guy and how he always said "meatballi," because I guess if you're saying pepperoni and salami and broccoli and all those other i words it would make sense to have meatballi as well, and Amber would always order meatballs because she loved so much to hear him shout out "Pizza! Meatballi!" It got to her so much that now *she* was even saying "meatballi" whenever she thought of meatballs, and I think I'll be doing it too. Who knows, maybe that guy in Chicago invented a whole new word and Amber was there to see it happen.

So of course we had to order a meatballi pizza, and then Dale asked for some napkini, and I passed the paper plati, and Amber said she wished the pizza had more sauci, and we were just having a grand old time speaking restaurant Italian, when who should come bounding up to our table but Beaner. Which is a word I don't use too much, "bounding," but it works really well for him. He'd just come in with a bunch of guy players from their West Lake game, which I guess they'd won because they were all in such a good mood.

"Yo! Wassup, ladies?" Beaner asked, slipping in beside me.

Amber kind of gave him the eye but Dale answered, "Not much. I'm Dale, by the way."

"My man," Beaner said, offering a fist for her to punch. "Beaner."

I was already getting all hot in the ears, although Beaner's boundingness didn't seem to bother Dale in the least, and Amber I shouldn't worry about because sooner or later she was going to have to figure out how to deal with Beaner and his being my guy, however it was that she did it.

"So how was your game?" I asked.

"Awesome." He shrugged. "Listen, I forgot to ask you before. You wanna go to the Valentine's Day dance? You know, the semiformal?"

Amber happened to be taking a big swig of pop when he asked this, and some of it actually came out her nose.

"That's great," Dale said, pounding Amber on the back. "Go for it, D.J."

"Oh." I handed Amber a big wad of napkini. "What, um, what do you wear to a semiformal?"

Beaner laughed. "I don't know! Wear my Hawley uniform — wouldn't that be awesome?" Meaning that T-shirt he'd made for the pep rally with the big HAWLEY 00 on the front.

I could feel sweat starting in my armpits. Amber and Dale were watching this like Beaner and I were a new sitcom they were checking out. "Um, seriously. What did people wear last year?"

He shrugged. "I dunno. I wore my granddad's tuxedo jacket and these really cool Hawaiian shorts."

"No way!" Dale said. "Me too!"

"You wore *shorts?*" I asked, just as Amber said, "You went to a *semiformal?*"

"All the seniors on the softball team went together. I had this tuxedo jacket I found in a thrift store. It was so great — it had sequins down the front and everything."

We all stared at her in shock. Well, Amber and I were in shock; Beaner was totally impressed. He slapped her hand, even. "That's. Totally. Awesome." He turned to me. "Anyway, lemme know. So, check in with you later." And then he was off, headed for the video games.

"You went to a *semiformal?*" Amber asked Dale again.

"It's no big deal. So what are you going to wear? Because it really shouldn't be a tuxedo."

A semiformal. What the heck was I going to wear to a semi-formal? I thought about asking Kathy Ott to help out with this little poser, but she'd already driven me to Minneapolis, not to mention all her help this fall with Mom, and fundraising for Win, and decorating our house . . . she'd done enough. She needed a Schwenk vacation. And it wasn't like Dad — or Curtis! — would have any ideas.

And it's not like I wanted to go to the semiformal much anyway. I'd never even been to a dance! At least the room would be dark. I knew that much about dances. And it didn't matter if you didn't know how to dance, because I know the kids in my school and it's not like any of them would ever make *Dancing with the Stars* except Kari maybe. Or Abby Halstaad.

Maybe Abby could help me with the dress. She probably had one already, knowing that kid. She could give me advice on how to go about getting one.

I was just beginning to make some peace with the whole concept of dress-shopping hell, and dance-going hell, when Brian reappeared. Literally. Saturday morning Curtis and I were sitting at the kitchen table doing homework when we heard someone pull in, crunching over the snow. Curtis saw the car first, and right away he shot a glance my way. I craned around to see, and there, heading for the spot where he used to park last summer, was Brian's blue Cherokee.

I leapt up and grabbed my jacket. What the heck was Brian doing here? Hadn't I made it clear that we shouldn't be talking anymore?

I tried to act cool, but I was still wiggling my boots on as I came up to him fussing with a camera.

"Hey," I said, smushing down my bedhead as best I could.

He smiled this crooked smile. "Hey. I, um . . . my dad wanted some pictures of the ramp. You know, to put up in his showroom. So he can be all 'look what we did.'"

"Oh."

"And I offered to take them. Save him a trip. That okay?"

"Sure. I mean, if your dad didn't want to drive over . . ."

"No, is it okay if I take pictures of the ramp?"

I swallowed. "Sure. Whatever."

We walked toward the house, our feet crunching on the snow. It was a really sunny day, bright enough to make you squint.

You know, Brian didn't have to come all the way over here and take these pictures. Mr. Nelson can drive to Red Bend and manage a camera just as well as his son.

"Is this light going to be okay?" I asked. Not saying what I was thinking.

He grinned. "Guess I should have waited for a cloudy day. That's what they say, you know, when you're taking pictures."

"That's what they say, huh?" I couldn't help it.

He grinned wider. "Yup. They do." He rubbed the back of his neck. "You want to go out with me?"

It took a second or two for the words to register. "What?"

"I said, 'Do you want to go out?' You know, to the movies or something. On a date, you know. Or, you know, two."

I almost plopped down on the snow, I was so surprised. "You're asking *me* to go out with you?"

"It's not that big a deal. Kids do it all the time. Drive to the movies, maybe grab a burger . . ."

"Ha. This is different, you know. What you're asking."

He nodded, serious all of a sudden. "I know. That's why I'm asking it."

"Brian, I've got a guy. I'm already going out with someone."

"So break up with him."

"I can't break up with him! He's my —" I tried to say *boyfriend,* but I couldn't. The word just wouldn't come out. "He's my friend. It'd be wrong."

"You don't like him," Brian said quietly.

"I do too!"

"Not like you like me. Not like I like you."

Well. *That* just sort of filled the yard for a couple of minutes, all the way up to the very farthest reaches of the atmosphere.

"I'm with Beaner," I said, finally.

"You don't have to be. You can change your mind."

"Are you going to change?" Looking him right in the eye when I asked this.

"I'd like to think I already have," he said, looking right back at me.

"Where have I heard that before?" I said. Well, actually I didn't *say* it. Actually I thought it up the next day. But I would have said it if I'd thought of it fast enough. Instead I just said something brilliant like "Oh, yeah?" Something you'd hear on a grade school playground.

"Really."

I nodded or shrugged or grunted, I can't really remember; what matters is that I didn't have a clue how to respond. We stood there for a few minutes feeling our noses freeze — mine was, anyway. Then Brian headed back to the Cherokee.

"Think about it," he said.

I nodded, and he drove away.

It wasn't until he'd left that I realized he hadn't even taken his pictures. But that hadn't really been the reason for his visit after all. Had it?

So that was something to think about all right, in those hours between ten p.m. and six in the morning that most people use for sleeping. For Brian to say he'd changed — I *had* heard that before. From him. But he'd never told his friends off before, the way he did that night at Taco Bell. So what if he was telling them off for making fun of Beaner instead of me — it was the same thing. He'd never smiled at me in public before. He'd never left a party for me.

And that business about how I didn't like Beaner — that was weird. That was weirder than weird. Was it really that obvious, like across-Taco-Bell obvious? And it wasn't even true ... Well, it was, kind of. It was true that I didn't like Beaner the way I liked Brian.

But with Beaner I knew what I was getting. So what if Brian made me feel like fireworks were going off inside me. He could also make me feel like a big fat clod of heartsick dirt. It was like he could take any emotion I had and make it ten times stronger. Which is great when it's happiness but pretty darn awful if it's anything sad.

So that's how my thinking would go, around and around. Only every once in a while we'd pause for a bit, my brain and I, at a little place called You're An Idiot. And while I was at that place, I'd list all the reasons I shouldn't be lying awake thinking about boys and boyfriends when I had so many more important things to do, when the world had so many more important problems. I was nothing better than those girls who stand in the girls' bathroom crying over their boyfriends. I was not that kind of girl, and I needed to shape up and start sleeping!

And then my brain would start puttering around once more.

That's how it went the next few days too, Dad and Curtis tiptoeing everywhere so I wouldn't bite their heads off like I did when Dad slapped me on the back Sunday morning and I yelled at him. Which just so you know is extremely unusual of me, and surprised Dad so much that he didn't even yell back; he just went out to the barn for a couple hours of peace. I even canceled cafeteria practice Monday afternoon because I just couldn't work up the energy, plus I was totally beat because it wasn't like my sleep Sunday night had been so fantastic either. All I could do, day and night, was think about what Brian had said, and how awful it would be to actually break up with Beaner, and how it would be that much worse if Brian then bailed on me afterward, after I'd made the mistake of falling for him yet again, because just because Brian said he'd changed didn't make it true, and how was I to know he wouldn't completely freak the first time his friends saw us together?

Then, just to make my life that much more fantastically wonderful, I walked into health class on Tuesday to find Ashley Erdel with huge red eyes and a pile of tissues, looking like her whole family had died.

"Hey." I settled next to her. "What's wrong?"

"I — didn't —" She began crying again. Of course the teacher didn't notice.

"You didn't what?" Ace health class? I'd kill that dumb teacher if this was the case.

"I didn't get in!" She pushed over a letter with a big red *W* logo. It was a pretty long letter, but she pointed out the word "deny." She knew where that word was right away.

"You didn't get into Madison?" I couldn't believe it.

"It's my SAT scores. I knew it." She dropped her head onto the desk.

I stared at the letter. It was all that "we regret," "many qualified applicants" baloney.

"I thought if I got my application in early enough . . . Oh, Madison! I *love* Madison!" Her shoulders began to shake.

"I'm so sorry . . . Oh, Ashley. Well, at least you got to play some basketball." But I didn't think that would cheer her up. And guess what? It didn't.

It was a pretty brutal game that afternoon against Two Geese. "Two Geese" is just about the coolest school name I've ever heard; when I was a kid I wanted to go to Two Geese so bad just so I could say it all the time. Now, though, I couldn't care less. I felt so awful for Ashley. Here she was playing basketball, taking tons of time that she should have been using to get even smarter, and in the end it didn't even help.

At least she was getting some playing time. Kari was back, with her ankle all taped and strict instructions not to rebound. But three other girls were out with strep — it's a wonder any of us were standing, really, so many kids were sick — and so Ashley went in almost right away, taking Kari's place while Kayla played point guard so Kari could rest her ankle a bit. Kari was guarding Two Geese 5 — see? Even that's cool, saying it like that — and so of course Ashley had to guard 5 when Kari was out, and it was great to see her using all the defense stuff we'd worked on, boxing 5 out and following her everywhere, sitting in her lap.

Only then Ashley planted a screen and 5 barreled into her and knocked her down, and Ashley didn't get back up.

For a moment my heart stopped. Last fall, you know, Win got face-masked, right in the middle of a PAC-Ten game. We watched it on TV, the whole thing, each minute dragging past like an eternity, time felt so slow, without him moving one tiny bit, as the players on the sideline stood in little huddles, some of them praying and some crying to themselves, the medics working as hard as they could, this huge crowd of medics and trainers, until finally after a whole lifetime, it seemed like, an ambulance crept out onto the field and they loaded him up . . .

Panic bubbled up inside me, all my hot game sweat suddenly freezing cold against my skin, as I watched Ashley lying there. Only she *was* moving, I told myself as I gasped for air. She was rocking back and forth and sobbing, clutching her arm to her chest.

They got her standing finally, her wrist already swollen and purple, her whole forearm wrong. Her mom was out on the court with her, and the trainer packed her arm with ice packs, every touch making Ashley scream it hurt so much, and her mom helped her out to their car, someone running ahead to pull the car right up to the entrance because you'd have to be dead not to know Ashley needed an ER stat.

Coach K gathered us up and tried to get us refocused on the game, but that wasn't going to work for me. Her right wrist was broken, her right hand — which is what always happens because of course everyone catches themselves with their dominant hand. Her writing hand. The same day she finds out her favorite college in the world doesn't want her, she breaks her wrist. So now the one thing she was good at, which is school, she wouldn't be able to do.

And it was all my fault. Because if I hadn't coached her so much, encouraged her to be so aggressive, she wouldn't have ended up doing something that a girl like Ashley should never, ever be doing, which is planting screens against Two Geese.

I was so upset that I missed six shots in a row, until finally Coach K pulled me out and told me to get myself in order. So I sat there on the bench with a towel over my head, wishing with all my heart I'd never started those stupid practices, and praying like crazy Ashley's wrist wouldn't end up as bad as it looked although it looked awfully bad.

At halftime we were down by seven. Coach K told us not to think about Ashley, that injuries are just part of the game and it wasn't anyone's fault, looking straight at me while he said it. But I knew that wasn't true.

As I was heading back on court he took me aside to say I needed to show some leadership.

"Leadership is what got Ashley hurt," I said, scowling at the floor.

"Don't you go thinking that. Leadership is what's going to win the game for her." Which was pretty lame of him, trying to turn it around like that. "D.J., you go out there and you show them what you can do."

Which, again, was pretty lame, but wouldn't you know I did. I guess all those years of Dad bossing me around, and Win, somehow got me trained to do whatever I'm told no matter what. It wasn't the best game of my life, that's for sure, but at least we won. And at the end of the game, Two Geese 5 found herself with a couple big bruises just for her.

It was pretty quiet in the locker room afterward. You could tell everyone was thinking about Ashley, how much she was hurting probably right that second. I felt awful, that's for sure.

Kari came over with a bunch of dollar bills and asked if I wanted to chip in on a teddy bear. Which is just the kind of good idea Kari always has — she's going to be such a great grownup — and I dug all of my change out of my backpack, some of it pretty linty, feeling a little bit better, just a tiny bit, because at least now I was doing something. Right then Coach K knocked and came in same as always for our post-game review, telling us everything we did right and for once kind of laying off on everything we did wrong, because of Ashley and all. A couple times he shot me a look I couldn't figure out at all, like he wanted to say something but not say it, if that makes any sense — it didn't make sense to me, anyway — and then as we were wrapping up, he asked me to come by his office.

Great. He did want to bawl me out, but just not in front of everyone. For what, though? I hadn't been that tough on 5 — was her coach complaining or something? Sheesh, grow up already. You should see how they play in the Big Ten. *Which I wasn't going to be playing in,* I reminded myself, but still. No need to be such a wuss.

Only when I went into the office, going through the little door from the locker room that's always so fun to use, like a secret passage or something, the first person I saw wasn't the Two Geese coach. It was Dad.

Dad never came to afternoon games — that's milking time. So what was he doing here?

Smut was hurt. That was the only thing I could think. Or maybe something had happened with Win, he'd re-lapsed or something — can you relapse from a broken neck? No, it must be Mom's back again. We'd warned and warned her, everyone from Dr. Miller on down to Curtis, but she'd lifted Win . . .

Only Dad didn't look the way he would if Mom was hurt, or Smut. I couldn't figure his expression out at all, actually, but whatever it was that had brought him all the way into *Coach K's office* couldn't be that bad. Not from his appearance.

Then I noticed, finally, the guy perched next to him on a folding chair: the coach from UW–Madison.

He held out his hand. "Good to see you again, D.J. That was an impressive game. Really," he added fast when my face fell. "It was very impressive. It takes a lot for a team to recover from an injury like that. You really pulled it together."

"Oh. Thanks . . ." It's a wonder my mouth worked at all, my brain was such a jumble. *What is the UW coach doing here?* He'd seen the game? How bad had I played? I couldn't even remember, I was so spazzed now. I needed a few hours alone just to review all my mistakes. How obvious had that business with Two Geese 5 been? Does a Big Ten coach want to see those sort of take-downs, or not? And on top of everything else, I was apparently supposed to be listening to what this guy was saying. What they all were. Which I was also blowing royally.

". . . too bad about Sasha Christensen." The UW coach was shaking his head. "I don't want Michigan State stealing another one of our players."

"Well, you go where you're wanted most," Dad put in, like he was some sort of sports commentator. "I mean, we all love Wisconsin, but from what I hear, they offered the Christensen girl a better package."

Coach K grinned at him. "You've been around the block on this, haven't you?"

"I'm just saying," Dad said. "You asked us here for a reason, dintcha?"

The UW coach leaned forward. "Yes, I did." He looked at Dad, and then at me. Right at me. "D.J., I'm here as a representative of the University of Wisconsin to offer you a four-year scholarship to Madison."

There was an extremely long silence. The three of them were staring at me, waiting.

To tell you the truth, brain-wise I was still back on Sasha Christensen. She'd been recruited five years ago, and this college coach knew all about it. Did he follow every girl player in the state? And remember them for years afterward? Had he been in this very office with Coach K half a decade ago, talking to the amazing Sasha Christensen?

"D.J.?" Coach K asked.

"You, um . . . wait." All of a sudden my brain caught up. "You just offered me a scholarship?"

Dad roared with laughter, and slapped me on the back. "That's what it sounds like to me, sport. Pretty exciting, huh?"

I sank into a folding chair. "Wow."

The UW coach grinned. "It gives me chills, every time. Twelve years I've been doing this, and I still . . . It's a pretty special moment."

"D.J.? You okay?" Coach K asked. Because the three of them were smiling and laughing, but I was just sitting there like a statue. "Don't worry about Ashley. This doesn't have anything to do with her. Athletic scholarships and academics, they're completely different."

I just got accepted to Madison. Accepted with one year of high school left. Without even applying. Without even taking my SATs. And Ashley, a girl who deserves college as much as anyone I've ever met, a girl who studies for fun, she hadn't. Instead they picked a girl who's never in her life cracked a book voluntarily and who wouldn't know a math formula if it hit her in the head. Whose only skill is dropping a ball through a hoop, and helping four other girls do the same.

There were thousands of kids dying to get into Madison who right this moment were probably going through the same heartbreak as Ashley, staring down at their rejection letters because the school didn't want brainy students, students who love to study and learn and make the world a better place, the school didn't want them half as much as it wanted ball players.

But do you want to know the really pathetic thing? I hadn't even thought about Ashley, not until Coach K brought her up. Now I felt twice as bad, if it's possible to double how bad I already felt. Because up until he said that, I'd been in an absolutely different kind of misery. Hadn't I made it clear to this UW coach that I didn't want to go to his school? I had to be polite, after all. I didn't say *your university sucks*. But couldn't he tell I was dead set against it?

No, I guess he couldn't. I guess he figured I was just being shy or something. Which I was, duh, but a heck of a lot shyer than he even figured because guess what, I was too shy to play. And now I was going to have to say that out loud. Say that truth. Admit to him, and to everyone in Red Bend — because you can be sure everyone would hear; knowing Dad, it'd be all over town by morning — that D.J. Schwenk didn't have the guts to play for Madison.

I knew, I knew already, that I would never be able to explain. Not in a way that anyone would understand. Never. All they would say, all they'd think, is that I was letting down the town. Letting down my school. Letting down the Schwenk name, and my family, and my brothers.

"This doesn't have anything to do, you know, with Beaner and all that?" Dad asked.

Oh, thank you, Dad. Because for a couple minutes there I'd forgotten about that whole heartbreak of Beaner and Brian. How I liked both of them so much, and how Brian was now asking me to choose. What possible training had I ever had, ever in my life, for that? None. I was actually better equipped to play Big Ten ball than to deal with having to choose between them.

"You okay, sport?" Dad asked. Sounding as worried as I've ever heard him.

"Yeah," I lied. "I just — I need some time. That's all."

"Of course." He gave me a little hug. "But you just need to know . . . I'm so proud of you."

I almost lost it, right then and there.

"It's a big shock," the UW coach put in. "I always think the girls will be expecting it, and I'm always surprised when they don't. You're a special person, D.J. Don't forget that."

Somehow I managed to smile. It felt like I had rigor mortis, that thing where your muscles freeze — that's how much strength it took. But I did smile at him, and not burst into tears. And I took the paperwork from him as he gathered up his stuff, and shook his hand, and even waved a bit as he walked out of the office.

The second the door clicked shut, though, I bolted for the locker room. But I hadn't made it half a step before Coach K grabbed my shoulder.

"What's the rush?"

"I — it's just —" What could I say? All I wanted, more than anything in the entire world, was aloneness. I wanted to be out of the office and away from Coach K, and from Dad who was beaming at me like I'd just won the lottery, which I guess in his eyes I just had. The girls' locker room was probably empty by now. I could sit there as long as I wanted, until the custodian kicked me out. Cry if I needed to — it sure felt like I did. Figure out what the heck had just happened.

Coach K eased me back into the folding chair. "We're not done yet," he said, giving me *another* weird look. He stuck his head out his door — his main door, not the secret passage one. The UW coach was still out there, talking to some woman, it sounded like. I really didn't care. *Just a couple more minutes,* I kept telling myself, like you'd tell a little kid who's about to lose it. *Just a couple more minutes.* I shut my eyes and took a deep breath.

"Pretty amazing, isn't it, sport?" Dad asked. He sounded so proud. Oh, God.

"Hi there, D.J." a woman said as the door clicked shut behind her. "Nice to see you again."

I opened my eyes to see the University of Minnesota coach settling herself in the folding chair.

She smiled at me. "I'm really glad I got a chance to see you play. I feel even more confident now about our decision."

No way, I thought. *No way. No way. No way.* I forced my face into another rigor mortis smile, a little one that wouldn't take too much energy, because it took all the energy I had just to sit there listening to that nice U of M coach talk. I didn't absorb everything she said. I couldn't. But I heard three words clearly enough. The words "delighted" and "full scholarship."

13
BARF SHOES

I HAVE NO IDEA HOW I made it home. Mom goes on and on about the dangers of drunk drivers, you hear all these public service announcements, but no one ever puts out announcements warning against hysterically sobbing sixteen year olds. I could have wrapped the Caravan around a telephone pole and I wouldn't have noticed except maybe to wonder why it was that I suddenly felt better. Because there's no way that totaling the car could've left me feeling worse.

At least I made it out of Coach's office okay. I shook hands with the U of M coach, and agreed that wow, it sure was a lot to absorb, and told Dad I was okay driving even though he was looking at me kind of funny. And K checked with both the coaches about when they needed answers. *I can answer right this second!*, I thought, but I didn't have the brainpower to get that out. Instead I just nodded and agreed with whatever they said, doing whatever I could to get out of there before I collapsed completely.

I made it out of the school parking lot, driving on autopilot, my brain spinning away with all these thoughts that I couldn't possibly organize. I didn't start crying until I was partway home. Then I couldn't stop.

I was still crying when Dad walked in half an hour later with Curtis. Who I'd been supposed to pick up, back before my life detonated. Whoops.

I haven't cried in front of anyone in I don't know how long. Okay, once last fall I cried with Win's coach's wife, that first night he was hurt. But I do my very best to go off alone whenever I get that way. Whenever I feel that pressure in my throat. So it must have been quite a shock for the two of them to walk in and find big tough D.J. sitting at the kitchen table in a puddle of boogers and tears, Smut pressed against my knee looking all concerned.

I couldn't see them because my head was down on the table, but I heard this long pause before the door clicked shut behind them. Curtis took a step back and slipped out of the room. Disappearing at the first sign of family tension.

"I'm sorry, sport. Coach K asked me to be there," Dad said. "Guess I shouldn't have come . . ."

"It's not that!" Only it probably sounded like "Iz — na — da" because I was crying so hard.

He patted my shoulder in an extremely awkward way. "Anything I can do to help?"

Which set me crying even harder.

Curtis walked back in and came over beside me. "Here."

I looked up: he was holding out a roll of toilet paper. I took a long sheet and blew my nose and wiped my eyes, then wiped off the table. "Thanks." At least it slowed my tears down, the combination of Curtis's niceness and Charmin. The tears didn't go away — I could feel them inside, just waiting to rev back up — but it gave me a bit of a breather.

"Guess you didn't want to go to Madison," Curtis said.

I laughed, a little non-laugh. "Guess I don't want Minnesota either," I said. Trying to sound casual instead of sobby.

All of a sudden the phone rang.

Dad picked up. "Hey . . . Oh, hey, Win . . . Yeah, you heard right. Wanna congratulate her?"

My face must have looked like a dynamited building, I started crying so fast.

"Oh!" Dad said. "Um, she, uh . . ."

"She's taking a shower," Curtis put in.

"Yeah. She's in the shower." Dad sounded pretty normal saying this, but he was looking at me like he couldn't figure out when the aliens had taken over his little girl.

I didn't care if I was full of aliens, I felt so bad. I just climbed the stairs to the bathroom — because it had been a good suggestion of Curtis's, doing that — with my face in my hands, the tears squeezing out between my fingers, and stood in the shower sobbing away, wondering if it was possible even to tell what was water and what was tears, and whether it really even mattered.

⑨ ⑨ ⑨ ⑨

School the next day — oh, boy. I don't know who told, Dad or Coach K or whoever, but every single kid and every single grownup in the building seemed to know. And all of them, it seemed like, sought me out to congratulate me, asking me which one I was going to choose. Over and over again, all day long. Asking which one I loved the most.

It was all I could do not to lose it, fending off everyone's congratulations and knock-'em-deads and advice on where I should go, advice completely and totally based on their own personal notions and totally un-based on me. All day long, whenever anyone said anything, anything about how fantastic Big Ten ball was, all I could think about was Tyrona's two missed free throws and how I'd never, ever, ever put myself in that position. Ever. No matter what.

Even Amber got in on it. Only she just assumed I'd be going to the U of M because then I'd be able to hang out with Dale's friends in St. Paul. It was like my part in this decision, my voice, had nothing to do with it — it was all about her happiness and how psyched she was to have me as part of their gang. Which wouldn't be a bad thing, necessarily — knowing Dale, those friends were probably okay — but I wasn't given a choice one way or the other. This wasn't the first time Amber's treated me like someone who should just tag along with her ideas, but it had never gotten under my skin before. Because this time it wasn't which movie to see or what the best F-150 color is; it was my *life*. Which Amber didn't seem to get. Didn't even seem to sense, really.

It got so bad, with Amber and everyone else, that I almost cut school. Walked out the front doors and just drove away. But I didn't, and you know why? For the simple, stupid reason that I had no other place to go. Any building I entered, even if it was the pizza place or the Super Saver or my very own home, was bound to have folks as ready to jaw my ear off as the population of Red Bend High School.

So really even more than cutting school I wanted to curl up and die. Okay, not *die* — I wasn't *suicidal*. But die temporarily at least. Die enough that everyone would leave me alone and not remind me every two seconds of how I was going to have to tell the whole town that I was really a big fat wuss.

At least Ashley wasn't in school. Apparently her wrist hurt so much that she stayed home. Kari swore Ashley had been really psyched when Kari had told her about me and Madison, which would have been great to hear except that it was just another example of how everyone was putting their own feelings in place of mine, and in place of Ashley's too, it sounded like. Because of course Kari was so psyched that she probably just projected all that psyched-ness onto Ashley. But it was still a relief to walk into health class and know I didn't have to face her.

I felt so awful that I skipped practice. I told Coach K I was sick, which was a lie unless you count emotional sickness, which I had absolutely.

"You doing okay?" he asked, studying me. "Must be a bit overwhelming."

"You can say that again."

"Me too, having two D-I coaches in my office . . . Jerry was expecting this, you know. He knew it was a long shot."

I looked at him blankly.

"You remember — Jerry Knudsen. From Ibsen College."

"Oh. Him. Yeah, well, I still want to go there."

K laughed, and patted me on the back. "Glad to see you're keeping a sense of humor."

He didn't even notice I was serious.

And then, just to make my day completely perfect, on the way out I ran into Beaner. Who I'd been avoiding all day for reasons you probably can figure out without too much strain.

"Yo! Rock star! Total congrats, man!" He jumped up on my back like always, the way that always cheers me up no matter what. Always did, anyway, until today. "So, you waiting to hear from Connecticut now? The Olympic team, maybe? Hey, what's wrong? You feeling bad?"

"Yes," I said. Because that's precisely how I was feeling.

"Yeah, well . . . It's probably not contagious." He gave me a kiss. "Man, you are sick."

"I know. I am."

Driving home, I couldn't help but wonder what Brian would think of all this. If he'd be able to understand what I was going through. He was a QB, after all; he knew what pressure was. Only he also knew how to handle it, a lot more than I did. He'd probably just say that of course I was good enough for D-I and I should just do it.

Which was exactly the advice I was already getting, and exactly what I didn't need to hear.

Then when I got home finally, I got another surprise, because sitting there at the kitchen table, wolfing down coffee and cinnamon buns, were the two farmers who'd helped us out right after Win got hurt.

Dad handed me a cinnamon bun. "Early practice there, sport?"

"Yeah, kind of." I eyeballed the farmers, trying to figure out what was going on.

"These fellas are going to manage the farm for a couple days," Dad said matter-of-factly. As if it was completely natural for him to turn his cows over to anyone who wasn't blood kin. "I'm heading over to Minnesota, you know. Spell your mother for a bit."

Then the three of them went out to the barn while I tried to sort this out. Dad hadn't even asked me. Normally — like every other time in my life up to now — he'd just dump all the farm work on me. Like last summer. He'd never call someone for help. Dad asking for help is right up there with Smut flying. That's what made it so amazing — trust me, I wasn't complaining or anything, I was just stumped — that he'd done it now. Without forcing me to argue about how important basketball is, and then feel bad about quitting like I'd had to do last winter after Dad's hip conked out. It was pretty nice of him, actually. Pretty darn thoughtful. Maybe meeting those two D-I coaches turned his head, too.

Or . . . Mom was in trouble. That was it. Really, it was a marvel she'd lasted as long as she did with Win. No one else could have done it. But finally she'd snapped too.

Still, I couldn't get over Dad calling those farmers. People might think helping is hard, but really that's the easy part; just look how good it makes people feel. Look how happy all those Red Bend ladies were about chipping in. It's the asking that's so painful. It takes real courage, real *strength,* to say you're not strong enough to do it alone. Mom must really be hurting for Dad to be so brave.

That night I refused to talk to Win. No matter how Dad glared, I didn't budge. My insides felt like a bunch of drinking glasses all stacked up, just teetering there, and I knew Win first thing would knock them down. I could hear Dad answering Win's questions — getting kind of irked himself, which was nice to hear, someone getting mad at Win besides me — saying he didn't know what I'd said to those coaches to make them so generous.

Which I didn't know either. Because hadn't I made it clear I wasn't interested? I'd been complimentary, sure, but I'd never said I was dying to go there and just couldn't wait.

Those words never came out of my mouth once. It was probably because the coaches felt sorry for us, because of Win and all. Maybe that's how strong Win's brainwashing is: he can even convince a school to offer up a ton of money just like that. It was almost worth calling the coaches just to ask what the heck they'd been thinking. Almost, but not quite.

Instead I listened to Dad reassuring someone — Mom, probably — that those farmers were fine and he'd be leaving right after morning milking. Poor Mom. She had all of Win's garbage to deal with, and all of Dad's as well . . . She definitely needed this break.

Only when we got home from practice the next day, there she was, puttering around the kitchen just like she always does, trying to figure out where Dad hid the frying pan.

"Well hello, honey," she said, giving me a big hug before I'd even had time to take off my coat. "Would you like some cocoa?"

"Ah, sure," I said, watching Curtis scoot upstairs to grab the shower.

Mom put two cocoas on the table and sat down. That in and of itself was weird. Normally she doesn't sit because she's too busy scooting. "So. I feel like we haven't caught up in a while."

"Yeah," I said, wondering when she'd turned into Oprah Winfrey. "Um, how's Win?"

"He's talking about going back to Seattle in June — can you believe it? And don't tell anyone, but I think Maryann is going to move out there too." She beamed. "Not that she's saying it has anything to do with him. Now, how are things with *you?*"

As far as weirdness goes, this conversation was already off the charts. "I'm not dating my physical therapist," I offered finally. If Mom wasn't going to bring up the scholarships, I certainly wasn't going there either.

Mom chuckled, then sighed. "Curtis is so worried about you, honey . . ."

"Curtis?"

"That boy . . . he insisted I come home. Really put his foot down. Isn't that something?"

It was all I could do not to burst into tears — burst into tears again — at the thought of Curtis looking out for me like that. Not that Mom would be able to help, but still, it was awfully considerate.

She squeezed my hand. "I heard Beaner asked you to the dance."

Great. Now I felt like crying twice as much.

"Don't you go worrying now. Dresses are *always* stressful."

"That's not it! Um — why, did you stress out about them?"

"Oh, yeah. I had shoes dyed to match for the senior prom. Had to go back three times to get the color right, you know." She sighed. "And then . . ."

"What? What happened?"

"Oh, nothing. Norman Boockvar — he was a basketball player, not that that matters. Anyway, he'd had a bit to drink, you know, and ended up throwing up on them."

I grinned — my first smile in days. "No way."

"Oh, yeah. And were they uncomfortable after that."

"You kept *wearing* them?"

"Well, I'd had them dyed. I wasn't going to just stop —"

"You danced in barf shoes? That's disgusting!" Man, did it cheer me up, hearing this story.

"And you know what? Last I heard, he was working in a shoe store." Which made me crack up even more. "So you see? We'll find you a dress now."

And — poof — my cheeriness was gone. I sighed. "It wasn't supposed to be like this, you know."

"Like what?"

"Like . . . so hard."

Mom had to smile. "You mean life is hard?"

"Yeah! I always used to think things like boys and scholarships, you know, and dances and stuff, that they were easy. That only lucky people got those. But I don't feel lucky at all."

Mom gave me a squeeze. "Welcome to growing up."

"You mean it's always like this?"

"No. It gets easier after a while. But you'll manage. Most everyone does."

☙ ☙ ☙ ☙

Only that's not how Win acted when I finally worked up the courage to speak to him.

Apparently it had been driving him so crazy that he ended up calling the coaches himself. And both of them said, at least according to Win, who's not like the most impartial person in the world, that they were really impressed with Mr. Jorgensen's tapes, how versatile I was and how I could take post or wing and was always willing to assist. How I was getting better at calling plays. How I got a bunch of girls to work out every day after practice. How I'd played football, and had been a total role model at football practice, which Coach Peterson told them when *he* called, which I hadn't even known he'd done, and talked their ears off even more than Coach K. Not to mention how us Schwenks are all so into sports, into helping each other and stuff, because apparently family support really matters even when the kid's not living at home, which is something I'm still having trouble figuring out. And both coaches heard, somehow, that I really wanted to go to their school.

"What?" I interrupted. "I never said that —"

Win snorted. "You can't go telling two different schools you like them best. How many times did I tell you that? Come on, D.J.! It's a real kick, I'm sure, getting these offers, but it's not right to lead them along like this."

For a while I just sat there gaping. "You think I said that? I never promised anything!"

"Of course you did. You told the Badgers coach you were really impressed with his program and that anyone would want to be part of it. He wrote it down. Your exact words."

"I was being *nice!*"

"That's not what people say when they're being nice. 'Great T-shirt' — that's nice. Saying 'I want to be part of your program' is something totally different —"

"That's not what I said at all! I would never say that!"

"So you were just jerking him around?" Why did Win *do* this? Take everything I said and turn it around like that?

"I wasn't jerking him around! I was just trying to say whatever I could . . . Listen, I don't even want to go to those schools. Okay?" There. It was scary, saying those words, but it was a huge relief too, to get if off my chest at last.

"What are you talking about?"

"Madison? Minnesota? I don't want to play D-I! I just want to go to some little school where hoops don't matter and there won't be any pressure —"

"Of course you want to play D-I," Win interrupted.

"Of course I *don't*. Just thinking about it makes me freak. There are tons of better girls —"

"Oh, yeah? You just had two coaches drive to *Red Bend* to offer you scholarships. You think they do that for everyone?"

"Win, you don't get it. *I don't want to play D-I.*"

"Jeez, D.J., could you stop being such a wuss?"

Which is why Mom walked in on my crying *again*, even though Win was still on the line. She took the phone away from me and shut herself in the office. Five minutes later she came out.

"Your brother is going to back off for a while," she announced. Guess Win's not the only bossy one in our family.

Which was one relief at least, one little tiny spot of good news. Because at the moment I was feeling about as bad as a human can feel and still manage to produce a pulse.

14
BEANER

THAT NIGHT I CALLED BRIAN. He was on my mind so much! I just needed to hear his voice. And — well, I wanted to hear a bit more. Find out if he really meant, you know, that thing about him changing.

So I called his cell, which I'll have memorized forever, and he picked up after only one ring. "Oh, man! It's so great you called!"

"Hello, this is D.J. Schwenk. Is Brian there?"

"Ha ha, very funny. Mucho congratulations, dude."

"For what?"

"For the scholarships! Listen to you, you're all like, 'Oh I've got so many offers I can't keep track of them all . . .' So where you going to go?"

I sighed. "I have no idea. I have no idea what I'm going to do."

"Because Madison and Milwaukee are really close, you know. We could hang together."

"'*Hang* together'? Who is this?"

Brian laughed. "You know what I mean. So. Have you, you know, made any decisions?"

"I told you, I have no idea."

"That's not what I was talking about," he said quietly.

"Oh. Listen, this is really hard for me . . ."

"What is?"

"You know. Being liked." I started to cry. I couldn't help it.

"Hey, it's okay . . ."

I gulped, trying to talk and sniffle and bawl all at the same time. "Do you know how many people watch D-I? I'd barf my guts out if I had to do that."

"That's not a good reason not to do it, though."

"Yeah, it is! People can die from barfing, like that thing you get when you're pregnant and you throw up so much that you *die* —" Which we'd just learned about in A&P and was now another thing I had to freak out about, whenever I ran out of all the normal subjects.

"No one dies from barfing, not anymore. They have IVs now and stuff."

"Like I'm going to go out on the court with an IV."

"Huh . . . Would knocking over an IV pole be considered an offensive foul?"

"Oh, totally. But you could use the pole to set one heck of a screen —"

"Uh-uh. Six inches max between player and pole."

"Six inches? You really think so?"

And that's where our conversation went from there, thank God, both of us laughing our butts off at the thought of a hoops game between two teams on intravenous fluids. Which makes absolutely no sense at all; I know that. But that's why it cheered me up, because it was so absolutely stupid. It cheered me up more than I'd ever thought I'd be cheered up again.

We had a game Friday of course, which we won no thanks to me because I was so hyperaware of how everyone in the stands was probably thinking that those two schools had both made a huge mistake. Plus I couldn't stop wondering whether there were any other college coaches in the crowd, sitting there all ready to judge me or talk to me or something. So my shooting went completely to pieces and don't even ask about my leadership. Then Saturday night Beaner and I went out with a bunch of kids. Beaner was in a great mood of course, and he was joking up a storm. The whole time, though, I couldn't help thinking about Brian. I so wished I could talk to him, talk right that second. Which was some kind of wishful thinking seeing as I was next to Beaner, his arm around me but nothing more. Which meant something. How could it not mean something, that I used to make out with Brian every chance the two of us got, but now I wouldn't let Beaner lay much more than a finger on me?

A couple times Beaner asked what was wrong, and Kari too, because I must have looked pretty bummed. And I was, I was totally bummed, because it was becoming so clear that Beaner and I weren't working out.

How do you say that? How do you tell a guy — a nice guy, not one of those guys in country songs who takes your guitar and your cowboy boots and your second-best dog — how do you tell someone who's sweet and funny and affectionate, and good to his little sister, and never ever mean, that every time you look at him, you're really thinking about someone else?

Would I want to hear that? No, I wouldn't. But I also wouldn't want someone looking at me with someone else on their mind, and in their heart. Just the thought gives me the shivers. Because you know what that means? It means that the person is dating you out of pity. And as low as I feel sometimes, I never want to get to that.

Finally I couldn't stand it anymore. I didn't know what exactly I was going to do, or when, but hanging around all those happy people, sitting next to happy Beaner, was just making me worse. So I said I was beat and my mom wanted me home, and headed out.

Beaner came along, walking me to the Caravan. "You okay? Really?"

I shook my head. "No. You, um, want to hang out a bit?"

So we sat together in the Caravan, our breath making clouds as we waited for it to warm up.

"I'm sorry about that crack about Minnesota," Beaner said. "If you want to be a Golden Gopher, go for it."

"No, it has nothing to do with that —"

"It's just — I mean, it is a funny name. 'Golden Gopher.' "

I couldn't help a smile. Beaner always makes me smile "It is. It's just . . . Oh, I don't know how to say this."

"Say what?" he asked, serious for once.

I studied the steering wheel. How do you possibly say it in a way that doesn't sound completely awful. *I really like you, but . . .* That's a lie. Because if you liked someone, you obviously wouldn't be breaking up. Or *I hope we can still be friends.* Yeah, right. Who'd want to be friends with someone who just broke up with you?

"If you can't find a dress, you know, don't sweat it —"

"No," I said. "That's not it. It's . . . I don't think I can go to the dance with you."

"Because you can't find a dress?"

"No! No, because . . . I don't think we're the best people for each other."

"What are you talking about? We have a great time together."

"Yeah, I know. I know we have a great time together. But I don't think we should see each other anymore."

"That doesn't make any sense," he said.

"I know it doesn't. I'm so sorry!" I started to cry. One of these days my eyeballs were going to just float away, I was crying so much.

"You don't like me?"

"No — I mean, yes, I like you. I like you a lot. I just don't . . . I don't like you that way. And I — and you deserve someone who does. Who likes you in that way too."

Beaner drew squiggles in the fogged-up windows. "You're serious."

"Yeah. I am." I wished I had some toilet paper. Where was Curtis when you needed him.

Beaner laughed a fake laugh. "I guess that explains why we never got very far."

"I'm sorry. I'm so sorry."

"You know, you're making it really hard for me to be mad at you."

I sobbed harder. He was so wonderful. For him to be joking, even at a time like this . . .

"Guess you don't have to buy a dress after all."

"Yeah." I sniffled. My sleeves looked like Smut had drooled all over them, they were so soggy.

"Okay. Guess I'll have to find someone else."

"I'm sorry," I said in a small voice.

"Yeah," he said. He climbed out of the Caravan. "See you around."

You know that feeling Christmas morning, when you wake up and tell yourself it can't be true because you've been waiting so long, days and weeks and months, and then you realize that this time it really *is* Christmas, and you leap out of bed because you can't wait to get downstairs? Well, now imagine the exact 180-degree opposite of that. That's how I felt Sunday morning. Oh, I felt awful. Plus now Beaner was going to have to find another date to the semiformal.

Jumbled in all that misery, though, was one other thought: at least now I wasn't faking it. Yes, I'd hurt him, but I no longer felt guilty about us going out. It wasn't a good thought, really — I mean, how can it be good to think you're no longer guilty? It just reminds you of how guilty you used to be — but it was different at least. Different enough to tweak the pain a bit.

I lay there for I don't know how long, feeling a tiny bit relieved but mostly just sorry for myself, picking at last night's conversation the way you'd pick at a scab, when my cell rang: Brian.

"Hey," I answered. Even the thought of Brian couldn't cheer me up.

"Hey yourself. I'm sorry about last night."

"What . . . ?"

"That guy. Breaking up."

Well, *that* got my eyes open. "How did you find out?" I managed at last.

"My buddy Carl Dietz. His cousin dates a friend of yours, Carrie something —"

"Kari." Tyler Dietz. Of course. Why should I even be

surprised the news would travel so fast, considering that everyone's life mission around here is to poke their nose in everyone else's business.

"So. I just wanted to check in, make sure you were okay . . ."

"Thanks. It was awful, you know. I never want to do that again as long as I live."

"I know. Although you know what my mom says? She says you're not truly human until you've had your heart broken and you've broken someone's heart."

"That makes me feel so much better."

"I know, it sounds pretty lame. But you know, I think she's right."

"I'll get back to you on that one." But already I did feel better, just a tiny bit, talking to him.

"So . . ."

"So . . . ?"

"So, were you — I mean . . ." He swallowed. "How are things, you know, between us?"

"I dunno. You tell me."

"Um, well, I think things between us might be okay. How about you?"

"Meaning, what do I think, or are things okay?"

"Yeah. Both of those."

I smiled. I actually smiled. "Yeah. Both of those."

"Hey! I just had an idea! You want to come over?"

"To your house?" I asked.

"No, to my private island. Of course to my house. I've got a ton of homework, and I was thinking, you know . . ."

"That you needed my help. Just say the word, Brian. I'm happy to help students who, you know, aren't as gifted as I am."

"Yeah . . . How are you with organic chemistry?"

"An Einstein. Totally."

So I checked with Mom, who of course asked if his parents were going to be around and made me call back to make sure, and he said yes and didn't even seem to mind, and I grabbed my backpack and headed over. Not so Brian and I could start making out, thank you very much — I'm not the kind of girl who breaks up with a guy and then goes kissing another guy the very next morning — but because even more than being an ex-kind-of-boyfriend, Brian was my friend. He was a good friend, and I really needed some good-friend company right now.

I'd driven past Brian's house before, and I knew already it was brand new and huge. But you couldn't tell from the outside just how huge it was. Right off the living room was a den big enough to hold hoops practice in. Half court, but still. With a ginormous TV and these huge puffy leather chairs all lined up, and his dad sitting there with a beer and the biggest remote I've ever seen, watching golf.

"Hey there, D.J.! Great to see you!" he called, not taking his eyes too far from the screen. Like anyone would miss anything in golf.

Then in the kitchen, which was about the size of our whole house, there was his mom — well, not in the kitchen exactly, but in this little room off the kitchen. Kind of like our office, only this one had really nice windows and a pretty view and all these books. And Mrs. Nelson sitting in front of a computer, typing away.

"Hello, D.J. Help yourself to anything in the fridge."

"Working on homework?" I asked. Trying to be friendly and all.

She smiled. "Yes, as a matter of fact. I'm speaking to the Western Wisconsin Lutheran Synod on Wednesday."

"Oh," I said. Luckily Brian dragged me away before I had to talk any more about *that*. Golf and Lutherans — no wonder he'd wanted me over.

We set up our books at the dining room table because Mrs. Nelson doesn't let him have girls in his room, I guess because she's not stupid, and I have to say it was awfully nice, awfully darn perfect, to work on A&P with Brian sitting right there beside me. Just one look at his organic chemistry made me super relieved I had A&P instead. We chatted while we worked, and I told him about how Mom's prom date had barfed on her shoes.

"You're making that up."

"Swear to God. She said she danced in them too. After."

"Ewww! Could you imagine? It'd be all like squishing between your toes . . ."

"Ew! Yuck!"

He laughed. "You're the one who brought it up."

"Well, yeah. But."

"My mom had a huge fight with her boyfriend at their prom. They broke up right in the middle of 'Freebird.' She had to walk all the way home. She says she still has the scars."

"Scars?"

"From the blisters . . . So. Which one is it going to be? Madison or the U of M?"

And *clunk*, there went my good mood. "Neither," I said with a shrug.

"Oh, come on. Really?"

"There are tons of other schools I could go to. This place St. Margaret's in Minneapolis has a really nice program it looks like, and there's this school Ibsen College that even gets to play Madison sometimes, in money games."

"Who wins?" Brian grinned.

"Ha ha, very funny. Anyway, I'm perfectly fine with D-III. I just wish everyone else was."

He sat there for a while, playing with his notebook. Gathering up those strips of paper that get left when you tear out a page. He sighed.

"What?" I asked. Because he looked so serious.

"I know you're fine with D-III. And you'll be an amazing D-III player, I'm sure; you'll probably be All-American. But you'll just stay the same."

"And that's bad?"

"No! You're great how you are. But with hoops, you know, you could go all the way. That's what people say."

"People say all sorts of crazy things."

"Yeah. But not about this." He stacked all the little torn-out strips into a pile, shaping a little pyramid with his fingers. "I know you're scared, and that's totally legitimate. But it's not reason enough not to do it. If you don't play D-I, you know . . ." He looked up and gave me a smile, this really adult-looking smile. Like we were both already wise. "You're brave, you know. You're a lot braver than you think. And if you don't do this, you'll never get the chance to become the player — to become the *person*, really — to become the person that this amazing girl named D.J. Schwenk was always meant to be."

15
ONE POSSIBLE BENEFIT OF A SUBSCRIPTION
TO *PSYCHOLOGY TODAY*

IT WAS DIFFERENT FROM WIN, what Brian said. Different from Amber and Beaner and Dad and Coach and all the college coaches and the Red Bend folks, those knock-'em-deads and make-us-prouds, everyone spouting their own personal reasons for me to play. For Brian to lay it on *me* instead . . . Maybe other folks had phrased it that way and I just hadn't heard, I dunno. But I sure heard it from Brian. And it made me feel about two inches tall. Because as bad as I felt about letting everyone else down, it felt worse to think I was letting me down. It felt — well, it felt like missing two free throws in front of ten thousand people.

So now I was nailed, basically. Completely nailed. Because if I decided to go for it and play D-I, I'd throw up in front of ten thousand people and die of dehydration. And if I didn't, I'd spend the rest of my life wondering who I could have turned into if only I'd had the guts to try.

And then, to make this experience that much more super-fantastic wonderful, when I got home Mom offered, like this was a huge gift I could never refuse, to take me out of school so we could shop for the semiformal. Which just reminded me that I *wasn't* going, and that I'd hurt Beaner.

Normally I view shopping with about as much enthusiasm as I do tearing my ACL. But skipping school meant I wouldn't have to see Beaner, or anyone else either. So I remarkably enough said yes, and Monday morning we dropped Curtis off at the middle school and then hit the road.

"So," Mom started, "it sure is nice to have some time together, just the two of us. I can't remember the last time we did something like this."

Never? I thought. But out loud I just agreed it'd been a while.

"What kind of dress are you thinking of? Cindy Jorgensen told me about this place that's got real nice ones."

Sure, I thought, *if you look like Kari.* "I dunno. Last year Beaner wore shorts and a tuxedo."

"Why am I not surprised? I swear, that young man is capable of just about anything —"

"We broke up." Which stunned me just as much as Mom, the words popping out like that. I guess my mouth decided to step up to the plate before my brain had time to intervene.

"Oh," said Mom. "Oh . . . Do you, ah, want to talk about it?"

"I think I just did."

"Well, yeah . . ."

"It was so hard! Why does breaking up with people have to be so hard?"

"Because it shows you care about the person. And that's a wonderful thing. I'm sorry, honey. It hurts, I know."

"But now he's going to have to find someone else and everything!"

"He'll be okay. There's not a girl in the world who wouldn't want — I mean, *most* girls — I mean, he won't have any trouble finding a date —"

"I know," I put in. Because she was trying at least.

She thought about it. "You know, why don't we go shopping anyway? You'll need a dress sometime, you know."

I wasn't so sure about that, but the alternative was turning around and going back to school. Any kind of shopping would be better than that.

"Um, where are we headed?" I asked when I finally noticed we weren't going in the mall direction at all. I'd been too busy listening to Mom's rehab gossip to pay attention.

"Mall of America," Mom answered like she said it all the time.

"What? That's like two hours away!"

"Well, that's where Cindy Jorgensen said the good dresses are. And I figured, you know, it would give us some good catching-up time."

Who *was* this woman? "Catching-up time?"

"There's nothing like a car trip, you know, for a real nice visit . . ." Luckily, though, she didn't push it, asking about Beaner or *Brian*, which would have been ten times worse. She just went back to talking about Maryann, the PT who might or might not be interested in Win, although the way Mom went on you'd think they were already married with a couple of kids. And I refrained from mentioning that my only other trip to Mall of America, with Brian, had ended with my very first kiss. I don't care how personal car rides get, I wasn't going into *that*.

The mall wasn't crowded seeing as it was Monday, but there were still girls there trying on dresses, all of them shorter than me — the girls I mean, although the dresses were too. It's not like stores spend a lot of time designing for someone who plays a pretty decent linebacker. Plus the dresses were all way too frilly or girly or trampy, which Mom said with a sniff, putting one back without even holding it up. Not to mention the prices. If we were going to spend that kind of money, I'd rather be getting, you know, basketball shoes. Something useful. Plus some of the other girls were getting in huge fights with *their* mothers, using words and attitude I couldn't imagine using ever, which made the whole experience just that much more delightful.

I stood there getting quieter and quieter, if by quiet you mean so depressed you can't even speak.

"You know, hon," Mom said, "this experience could be kind of fun, if you let it . . ."

Which made me feel so much better, knowing I was flunking our family bonding experience.

Although you know what? Just five minutes later as we were walking around, Mom looked in the window of a store we hadn't even thought to go in and saw a dress. A pretty decent one.

"It won't fit," I said, just to establish that baseline.

But she made us go in anyway, and sure enough it didn't. But right there on the next rack, underneath a big red CLEARANCE sign, was one that did. It was really simple and dark, and pretty short — shorter than my uniform shorts, which are really long, but still. Mom pointed out that the length was perfect for awards banquets, and parties in the spring or summer even, if I ever happened to get invited to any of those.

"Could I wear my b-ball earrings?" I asked. Which made her laugh, and she said she wouldn't wear anything else. And *that* good mood got us through finding shoes, which of course couldn't have heels because guess how much I like those. At one point I asked if I could just wear tennies and she shot me a look. But we managed to find a pair that weren't expensive at all, and then she picked out pantyhose, which I started to squawk about until she said I'd get horrible blisters otherwise, which shut me right up. Then as we were paying, Bill called Mom's cell and found out where we were and said we *had* to stop by the U of M, and Mom said she'd never seen the Barn, and before I could object, Bill said he'd meet us there.

⑤ ⑤ ⑤ ⑤

So with her driving and me navigating, we made it there finally, Mom doing her isn't-this-nice thing as we circled the campus. I couldn't tell if she was trying to get me to like the U of M or was just poking around for her own curiosity, but either way it was best to just keep my mouth shut and wait it out.

Bill walked us into the basketball arena, asking Mom about our shopping because he hangs around girls enough to know the right questions about stuff like that. Luckily there was just a cheerleading practice going on at the moment, a couple cheerleading groupies sitting in the stands, but not hoops practice and no hoops coaches, either, to freak me out more than I already was. Mom just stood with her mouth hanging open, taking it all in.

"It's so . . . so . . ."

"Big?" I offered.

"So *loud*. What's it like when this place is full?"

Bill and I both laughed. "Really loud," I said.

"I'd think so . . ." She settled herself into a chair, staring around.

I walked a ways away and sat down myself, picking out landmarks. There was the spot where Tyrona missed her free throws. There was the seat where I'd watched her. There's where I'd almost thrown up.

I swallowed, my stomach heaving again just at the memory. It didn't matter what Brian said about my potential. Nothing — nothing — was worth feeling this sick for four years straight.

Bill squeezed beside me, squishing himself into a chair. "How ya doing?"

"Okay."

"Win called me, you know. He thinks you might really bail on those offers."

I shrugged. "He thinks right."

"I was really looking forward to hanging out with you. The media people were going to make a big story out of it and everything, us both being varsity and all."

"I'm sure you'll get famous some other way."

"Aw, that's not what I meant." He looked across the arena. "You know, preseason my freshman year, I was so nervous . . . I spent more time in the bathroom than I did on the field."

"Throwing up?" I asked.

"Oh, no. The other one. I was in that stall every ten minutes, it felt like. The trainers finally had to give me a special diet just to keep my weight on. That's how bad it was."

I turned to look at him. "You're kidding."

He picked at a hangnail. "Why do you think they call me Milkshake?"

"*What?* That's just because of the farm, and Wisconsin —"

"Yeah, right."

I stared at him. "You never told me this."

"You think it's something I'd brag about?"

"You don't seem scared."

"Huh. You should see Aaron before games — his hands shake so much, I have to lace his cleats."

"*Aaron?* Nothing fazes him."

"You don't get it, D.J." Bill shook his head. "*Everyone's* scared. So scared they can't sleep sometimes. Or eat. Or keep their weight on."

"Then why bother playing?" I asked. It was a whisper, this question.

"Because. You love the game. You love the people you play with. You love winning, maybe. You love that one moment when you get it right . . . I dunno. Why do you play?"

"Because," I whispered, "it's who I am."

"Sounds like a good reason to me."

"But what about all those people watching?"

He grinned. "I wear a mask, you know. It helps that no one can see your face."

Which was something to think about, all right. It would definitely relieve the pressure, that icebergs-in-your-belly feeling, if no one could see who you were. Or if you *thought* that at least. Maybe I should just play as someone else. Ha.

Although maybe . . . maybe . . . that wasn't such a bad idea.

◎ ◎ ◎ ◎ ◎

The next day I couldn't wait to get to health class, which was a first for me, actually looking forward to that snoozefest. Ashley was back of course, taking notes as best she could with her left hand. Luckily second semester doesn't matter so much, not for seniors. The two of us had talked, finally, about Madison, and just like it usually happens with awkward conversations, it turned out to be not so bad. Kari had been right that Ashley was psyched for me, and also psyched that she'd just gotten into UW–Oshkosh, with a real sweet financial aid package too, and now had big plans to work her butt off at Oshkosh for a year and then transfer. So really — she explained to me — it was better this way, because she could still go to Madison but save a bunch of money in the meantime.

"Are you going to play?" I'd asked. I was serious, but Ashley just laughed.

"They're really good! Oshkosh is D-III, yeah, but they're still really good." She thought about it. "Although, you know, it really was fun, being part of a team."

"You could be a manager," I pointed out. "A student manager. They're really important, helping out with practices and stuff. And tracking stats too, I bet."

Ashley's head came up. "Statistics?" she asked. Her eyes got wide. "You mean like . . . math?"

Anyway, the day after my Mall of America / Big Talk with Bill trip, I was back in school same as always, and same as always I plunked down next to her and asked how she was, and same as always she said okay.

"Great. Hey, listen. Remember winter break when you were talking, you know, about how I should pretend I was someone else?"

Ashley nodded. "That *Psychology Today* article."

"Yeah, that . . . Anyway, um, what were you talking about?"

Ashley lit up, totally psyched to put her enormously-large-even-if-Madison-doesn't-want-it brain to work. "You know how you tell Kari what to do during games?"

I nodded, surprised she'd noticed. Maybe Ashley had more hoops sense than I'd thought.

"So you know what you *should* say, right?"

I shrugged. "Yeah, sometimes."

"So what if instead of telling Kari, you just pretended you were her? Not *Kari* necessarily, but someone like her? And you just spoke out loud while pretending to be that person?"

I thought about it. Ashley had a point, kind of.

"Give her another name, even. Call her Darlene or J.J. or . . ." She frowned to herself. I mean, name-wise Darlene and Joyce and Schwenk are all pretty pathetic starting points. "Darly or Darey or Doyce —"

I held up my hand. "What did you just say?"

"Doyce? Darey?"

I frowned. "Did you hear me? When we were practicing?"

"Hear what?" She started to look hopeful. "When?"

"Nothing. That's weird. Darey . . ."

All of a sudden the teacher was right there in front of us. "Excuse me. Do you two have something to say?"

"We were just wondering about homogenization," Ashley answered, not missing a beat.

"What?" the teacher asked. *What?* I thought.

"Because of the reported health risks of homogenized milk." Ashley made this *You didn't know that?* face. Gosh, she was smart to think so fast.

"But if you didn't homogenize milk, you'd get tuberculosis," the teacher said smugly.

"No, it's pasteurization that prevents TB," Ashley said. Without adding *You stupid moron* like she could have.

"Oh, I'm pretty sure I know my dairy."

Only there were a couple other kids in the class who knew homogenization from pasteurization for crying out loud, and they started arguing with her until she went to a textbook to prove her point and then had to argue about why the book was wrong as well, and in the end she made Ashley move her seat, which was probably the first time in her whole life that Ashley got in trouble just for being right.

I barely noticed, though, because I was too busy thinking about what Ashley had just said.

Remember way back when the two of us first started working together, when I told her most people have a little thing, a ritual, they do for free throws? Well, ever since I started playing ball, when I'm standing at the line I say to myself — which you'll probably understand given that I learned to play from Win and Bill — I say: "Dare me? I dare you. Dare me? I dare you. Dare me? I dare you." And then I shoot. Every time. Six bounces, six little sentences, swish. (Well, *hopefully* swish.) And that word Darey, the way Ashley said it, just struck me as being awfully close to Dare Me. It was like, *Snap!* I'd say it was an omen only I hate that word because I saw that movie on TV once and had nightmares for years afterward, how can any omen be good after a creep like Damien takes it over?

Anyway, now that Ashley had described it like that to me, now that I had a *name* and everything, I couldn't get Darey out of my mind. What would it feel like to be playing, but not as D.J.? Sitting in A&P — which usually I love, but today Mr. Larson might as well have been speaking in Chinese, I was so not paying attention — I kept picturing myself on the court as point guard. Each time my stomach would clench just like it always does. But then I'd say to myself it wasn't *D.J.* out there; it was just this other person I was playing, like an actor playing a part, the part of someone who's really good at shouting instructions and showing leadership because that's just who she is.

Sometimes it didn't work. No matter what I told myself, my gut would clench and my hands would sweat, my heart would start hammering away . . . And if that's how I responded, just sitting in A&P, to the *idea* of point guard, what would I be like in a game? And I'd decide that this whole Darey thing was an extremely ridiculous idea.

But then I'd try again. And sometimes, you know, sometimes I could actually get my head there, into Darey's mindset, pretending for a minute to be someone who was actually confident.

I really, *really* wished I could talk to Brian. See what he thought about it. After all, just on Sunday he'd been telling me how I needed to let myself be the person I needed to become, however it was he'd phrased it — he'd said it a lot better than that. And isn't this exactly what the whole Darey business would accomplish? Darey could be that person!

But of course I couldn't talk to him. For one thing, you can't make cell calls during school — it's like an automatic detention. I even thought about cutting lunch and driving over to Hawley just to track him down. Which was an even worse idea because cutting wouldn't just get me detention; it would get me benched. Plus walking into Hawley's cafeteria — no matter how much Brian said he'd changed, that's really not fair. That's like taking off a little kid's training wheels and telling him to bike a marathon.

But I still wanted to do it. Because I really needed Brian, of course. But I also very, very much did not want to eat in the

Red Bend cafeteria.

Oh, Beaner. Every time I thought about him, I felt sick. He hadn't yelled at me or anything! Or cried or something — I mean, *I* cried, which I was very embarrassed about, but he'd just sat there like a stone. Like it hadn't even hit him. Which meant that later it probably hit him twice as much.

I would have skipped lunch altogether, but I was starving. And there was no place else to go because I'd stopped those Spanish reviews sessions with Mrs. LeVoir once it was clear I was as good as I was ever going to get, which I now really regretted — stopping, I mean; I don't regret sucking at Spanish, because that's just a waste of energy. But it wasn't like I could sit at Beaner's table anymore; I'd get juice dumped on me at the very least.

So I went through the line like always, not looking at anyone while at the same time trying to spot an empty table somewhere, a corner or something, where I could gulp down enough food to get me through the game.

Only just as I was paying, I heard my name.

"Over here," Amber called, pointing to a space across from her.

Oh, it was so awesome to see her! Like catching sight of Santa Claus after you've stopping believing.

"What are you doing here?" I asked, trying not to look as relieved as I felt. "You're never here!"

She shrugged. "I figured today you probably needed some

girl power. You gonna eat that fruit salad?"

She'd heard. She heard about Beaner and she made sure to be here, just for me. For a moment I couldn't speak or I'd have started crying. "Um . . . just the pineapple. You want the rest?"

And that's how our conversation went, because when you're sitting in a high school cafeteria trying not to blubber in front of your best friend, it's best to focus on canned tropical fruits. And then Kari of all people asked if she could join us, like *we* were the popular ones and she wasn't. And Amber said only if she wasn't stingy with *her* fruit salad, which Kari promised not to be.

"It's, like, so loud over there," Kari said, nodding toward the guys' table on the other side of the room. "You can't even hear yourself think."

"I don't think they do much thinking," I put in. Not meaning to be mean about it, though we couldn't help laughing.

But then right in the middle of our laughter we heard "Yo, wassup, dudes?" and there was Beaner. He had a girl with him too, a freshman who wouldn't look me in the eye.

"Hey, Beaner," Kari said. "We're going to hang here today. Just some girl time."

"Hey," I managed.

Beaner nodded. "That's cool." He looked at me. "Hey. Have a great game tonight. Okay?"

"Um, you too," I said. I even managed a smile.

Beaner grinned back, and then he was off, trailed by that little freshman.

"What the heck was that all about?" Amber asked. She sounded disappointed.

"You okay?" Kari asked me.

I shrugged. "Yeah, fine. Whatever."

Kari watched me for a minute — they both did — and then they started talking about this big scandal with this actor and a car or something. They both seemed to know every single detail, but I'd never even heard of the guy. And even if I had I wouldn't have cared, because my brain was too busy trying to figure out what had just happened.

Beaner wasn't upset. Or if he was upset, he hid it really, really well. Here it was only three days after our breakup and he was already seeing someone, going on with his life. Not even mad at me. Which meant, I guess, that he was a really mature kind of guy.

Or . . . it meant our relationship hadn't mattered. Which, much as I hated to think it, was probably a lot closer to the truth. It's not that Beaner didn't *care* about me. He cared enough to wish me a good game, after all. To say hello. But if it had been me and Brian — when it *had* been me and Brian — we couldn't have been in the same room together. The same building. And the fact that Beaner and I were still okay, well, what did that say about what the two of us had had together?

You know what it said? It said we didn't have much. All those times I'd had a pang because I didn't feel that spark . . . well, I guess Beaner didn't feel a spark either. Maybe we'd just gone out because we were such good friends that we thought we could take it further. Take it further kissing-wise (although nothing more than kissing, which tells you something), and further emotionally too. Although not much further that way either, it turned out. Which is too bad, because I'd like to think I'm worth more than that. That Beaner and I both are.

That night we played Bonnelac. The boys did too, of course. It was going to be a really rough game for them because Bonnelac has this super hotshot sophomore who's already being scouted by a bunch of schools, and I tried to send good thoughts Beaner's way, get him a boost somehow; it was the least I could do. But it was a pretty rough game for us as well, especially for me because I was working so hard with Darey.

I sat alone on the bus the whole ride over, trying to get my head there. It's really hard for me to get my head anywhere, especially when it comes, you know, to even thinking about expressing myself. And once we were playing, with Kari as point as always and me at center, I tried to keep my eyes extra open for things that a good leadership-type player might want to note, like how Bonnelac's 40 couldn't pass to her left. Then I'd panic like always and think that Kari should say something, and then that I should say something to Kari so she'd speak up, and then I'd think, *Wait a minute. Darey can do that!* And I'd remind myself that I was playing the part of an amazing girl basketball player and that this character needed to *lead*. And then Darey, using my mouth — it was crazy, it was like I was outside my body observing this person do stuff — she'd tell Kayla to stay all over 40's right side so that 40 would blow her passes.

As you can see, this was an extremely complicated and roundabout way of conveying one little piece of information, so it didn't happen all that frequently. Most of the time I blew it like I always do. But at least I didn't spend the whole game wishing I could put a paper bag over my head and hide in the boys' locker room. And afterward Coach K mentioned how much more assertive I'd been. Which was a stretch, the "much more" part, but I wasn't going to argue.

I worked on Darey at practice too, for the rest of the week, trying over and over to get my head into hers. I started whispering to myself, things like "Come on, Darey, step up!" Just like Coach K does, which I didn't even realize for a while, duh. And then more than whispering, like when we were practicing this new play with Jess, and three times in a row she got herself boxed in. If she couldn't keep herself open with a freshman guarding her, how the heck would she manage against Hawley? Which Darey pointed out, getting kind of sharp with her, even.

Jess stared at me like I'd lost my mind, but Kari and Kayla let out this huge whoop and started applauding. Even the freshmen were cheering, and Coach K came over and felt my forehead, making this big show about how I must be sick and maybe we should call an ambulance, while I stood there wishing I could melt through the floor.

Ashley was sitting in the bleachers, laughing her head off. Since our UW–Oshkosh talk, she'd come to every practice, doing her homework in the bleachers but watching us too. Figuring out how to be a short little genius student manager. "Way to go, Darey!" she called out now.

Kari looked over at her. "What are you talking about?"

Ashley stopped laughing and bit her lip. She looked totally embarrassed.

I sighed. "It's okay. You can tell them."

So Ashley, after asking me four or five more times if it was really okay to spill the beans like this, finally described *Psychology Today* and her brother's orthodontist appointment, that article about shyness and how pretending that you're someone else, the way actors do, can actually help you overcome it. "And so that's what D.J.'s doing. She's acting, well, like . . ."

"Like a real basketball player," I put in.

Coach K was nodding to himself. "You know, that's not a bad idea there."

"But who *are* you?" Kari asked. "I mean, if you're pretending to be someone, who is it?"

I shrugged. "No one in particular. I just think of this person and have her act, you know, the way a real ballplayer would."

"What's her name?" Kayla asked.

I hesitated. What harm could it do? Heck, it might even help things. I swallowed. "Darey."

"Oh!" Kari clapped her hands. "That is so cool! You're — you're — you're Dairy Queen!"

16
DAREY QUEEN

WIN DIDN'T CALL HOME FOR the rest of the week. Or if he did call home, he didn't ask for me. Or if he did ask for me, Mom didn't put him through. That's probably what happened, that third one. Whatever the explanation was, I sure wasn't complaining. Even though it had only been a week since I'd met those two coaches, Win made it sound like I was holding up the coronation of a president or something. But I couldn't answer, because . . . well, because of a lot of things.

I was talking to Brian now, talking a lot. Every night doing homework — which we did get finished sometimes, just so you know — we'd gab away for hours. I told him about Darey and Ashley and *Psychology Today,* and the two of us busted a gut about how I hadn't even noticed Darey and Dairy sound the same. And he agreed it was totally logical that I'd be able to open my mouth as someone else a lot more easily than as plain old D.J.

"I still don't want to play D-I, though," I put in.

"But you're thinking about it," Brian said.

"No, I'm not!"

"Yeah, you are. Because if you weren't, you wouldn't have brought it up."

"Um . . . maybe," I said in a real small voice.

There was a bit of a silence. Brian sighed, hard. "D.J.? I have . . . I have a confession to make."

Well, you hear a phrase like that and your heart just stops. And your brain starts going a million miles an hour with *He's got a girlfriend . . . His father hates us again . . . Smut's asked to move in with the Nelsons.* "Uh, okay."

"You are going to bust me so bad for this, I just know it . . . I think I'm going to UW–Milwaukee. And, well, they don't have a football team."

"*What?* But you're an awesome quarterback! How could you not play —"

"That's the thing. They've got a club. They just play for fun. I can still QB but it won't, you know . . . it won't be all that pressure."

There was a long silence while I thought about this. I swallowed. "Can girls play?"

Brian started laughing so hard that he dropped his phone. Then he started coughing, he was laughing so much, but he couldn't stop. Finally he calmed down enough to make me swear I wouldn't *ever* go to UW–Milwaukee and show him up. Which, you know, I could never do, because there's no such thing as a club athletic scholarship. The Nelsons might be able to pay for college, but that was the whole point of my playing hoops: it was the only way I could afford it.

I still couldn't help getting a pang, though, at how much fun club football would be.

And I have to admit that it was pretty amazing to hear Brian acknowledge that he wasn't so, you know, lionhearted. (Although when you go to a zoo, all the lions do all day long is sleep their heads off and flick their tails, so why anyone would ever want a heart like that I can't understand.) To learn that he was also freaked about college ball. As wild as it had been to hear about Bill. Or Aaron, who's as big as a house and could tackle a zoo lion all by himself, to hear that even he gets the shakes. It opened my eyes, I guess you could say. Because Brian saying I was brave meant an awful lot more, you know, now that we both knew he kind of wasn't.

Although Brian *was* brave in his own way, braver than I'll ever be when I think about how much courage it took for him to come to our second Hawley game — which had a huger crowd than normal even because this was Hawley's big chance to show that losing to us had been a fluke and our big chance to prove we actually were better even in our tiny beat-up gymnasium — and not only to come, but to sit in the Red Bend bleachers. With the quote-unquote enemy. He sat next to Mom, even. Which was extra particularly brave of him because Mom was so psyched to finally get to see me play Hawley in person that she was probably the loudest person in the building. I noticed Brian didn't open his mouth much, at least not when I was looking. Maybe he figured that being next to Mom he didn't need to. Or he was just being neutral, which is an awfully smart position to take if you're from Hawley and sitting on the Red Bend side.

Thanks to Kayla's bruised tailbone, and Kari and all those strep victims, our benchwarmers now had more experience, and we'd really gotten good at that draw-out-the-clock-and-wait-for-an-opening offense. It was pretty cool, actually, that with Kayla and Kari back, now we could go both ways, full-court press or wait and see, and it was nice to watch Hawley trying to figure out which one it would be, messing with their heads like that. Darey liked that a lot. Plus 23 was parked on the Hawley bench with her leg in a big black Velcro cast. The sight of her shouldn't have made me happy, but it did, I won't lie. Though I tried right away to think good thoughts about her because otherwise that's just asking God to nail you next.

Then, about five minutes into the game, Kari gave me a nudge and nodded toward the doors. And guess who was coming in? Not Beaner, duh, because he was playing Hawley away. And not the Otts, or Amber and Dale, or anyone like that, because all those people were already there. And no college coaches either, thank God. No, it was Dad. Pushing Win.

I was so surprised, so totally shocked at the sight of Win in his wheelchair in the Red Bend gymnasium, giving me his little SCI wave, that I missed a pass. Missed as in it flew right past my face and I never even blinked. It was probably pretty funny, now that I think about it, Red Bend's star player standing there with my mouth so open that I probably could have caught the ball just with my lips.

Of course Win saw this and grinned, and that got me back into the game, more or less. Only I blew my next couple shots so you can see how back into the game I actually was. It didn't help that I could hear the whispers, actually *see* the news spreading through the crowd: *Win Schwenk is here!* Win is pretty much the best football player in the history of Red Bend, and as you know every single person in town has been following his story nonstop since the accident. So probably no one even saw me blow it; they were all so busy trying to catch a glimpse of my big brother.

We won. The suspense is killing you, I know, so I'll just go ahead and blurt it out. We won by ten points, which is the most any Red Bend team, girls' or boys', has beaten Hawley since our two schools started playing. Which only four different people told me afterward, so it's not like anyone keeps track. And you can go ahead and say it was 23's torn ACL all you want, but I'd like to think it was us. Us plus Win. Win and Darey.

Because it turns out Darey really enjoys basketball. Not that she's Magic Johnson, but at least she's not running around with a mouth all covered in duct tape. It was head and shoulders better than how I usually played. Head and shoulders and maybe even kneecaps. Sure, I freaked sometimes, but instead of just spiraling down into a spazzed-out lump of self-pitying D.J., right when the freaking started I'd notice a little thing, maybe only that Kari needed to switch, and then think of Darey. Then we'd speak up, Darey and me together, which would calm my spazzed-ness enough to keep playing without totally despising myself.

So you can see why I say that Darey won the game for us. Because even if she didn't, she kept me from losing it — losing the game and losing it, period.

And then afterward . . . wow.

There was a time not too long ago when Win wanted to die — not as in "Oh, I'm bummed," but literally die. Because he believed his life was over, so why not make it official. And for a while after that he didn't want anyone seeing him in a wheelchair, seeing him disabled in any way. And yet there he sat as the bleachers were emptying, shaking hands with hundreds of people, accepting their best wishes like he'd been born to the role. Talk about a natural leader.

Ashley found me in the crowd and stood on tiptoes to whisper in my ear. "Do you think — um, would your brother mind signing my cast?"

I cracked up. "Absolutely. He'd love it."

And he did love it, signing away with his special big-grip pen. You should have seen Ashley's face when he asked how it happened and she got to say "Setting a screen." And then she said what a good coach his sister was, and Win grinned at me and said he already knew.

Brian came over as well. Most of the Hawley fans had left by then, not wanting to linger for obvious reasons. But Brian just stood there waiting for the fuss to die down as everyone and their brother squeezed around Win, saying how delighted they were to see him, and how much they were praying, how good he looked. Which he did, I guess because he was happy. Brian didn't even flinch when some Hawley kids started giving him a hard time. He just said he needed to speak to someone and he'd catch up with them in a few minutes. How do you like that?

I could see Win frowning as Brian came up to him, which you can understand seeing as Win had spent the past half-hour trying to place Sunday school teachers and fourth grade coaches and old girlfriends' parents.

"It's Brian Nelson," said Dad. "His father got us that van, and built the ramp." This from a guy who a year ago couldn't admit that his kids helped him milk. Actually, he probably still can't admit that. But he sure seemed happy with the Nelsons.

Win took Brian's hand. "I can't thank you enough for all your generosity."

"Hey, no worries," Brian said with a grin.

"You treating my sister right?" Jeez, Win! He still had Brian's hand too, like he wouldn't let go if Brian answered wrong. Talk about embarrassing.

"Doing my best," Brian said, smiling at me. "Doing my best."

Seeing that smile, my embarrassment pretty much vanished. *And* my happiness at winning the game — the *second* game, ha. And my satisfaction with Darey, Ashley's whole brilliant idea that seemed to be working out so well. And all my worries about college, which usually hung around nonstop waiting for a free moment to pop out and drive me insane. Instead, right at that moment, all I felt was crazy love for Brian. If he'd taken me in his arms and dropped me into one of those kisses, the kind you see in pictures from World War II, I would have been totally into it, and kissed him right back. Right there in front of everyone.

But I didn't. Instead I called the U of M.

Which probably doesn't make sense, those thoughts together like that. Because it's not like I wanted the U of M to kiss me . . . although maybe I did. Because when you think about it, a scholarship is really kind of a great big swoopy movie-star kiss.

I know, I know: I wasn't calling the University of Wisconsin. Even though UW's in *Madison,* which has Mica and great haircuts, and I'd be representing my *state.* And Brian would be less than two hours away. And Ashley still meant to end up there and then she could help me with my homework. And I really did like the Madison coaches, and the classes were probably okay too, which I probably should have been thinking about, but I wasn't.

But the University of Minnesota, you know, has Bill and Aaron, which are two enormous pluses and I don't mean their size. And it's closer to home, to Red Bend, which is something I didn't think I'd care about, but it ends up I really care a lot. And I really, really liked that coach, and Tyrona, more even than the folks at Madison. Even more than I liked Mica.

It was a tough call, I admit. Really tough. Kind of like having to choose between Beaner and Brian, which had only been about the worst experience of my life, and now here I was a couple days later on yet another torture rack of big decisions.

Not to mention that I was calling at all, given I spent the past two months convincing myself that I'd never in my life play D-I ball.

You want to know what changed my mind? That trip to Brian's house.

All summer I was really hurt about how he never invited me over to his house. All summer, and fall. Then once I got inside and saw how huge and fancy it was, I was totally mortified about how bad our rundown farm must look in comparison. Of course that's why he'd never had me over! He was protecting me. He didn't want me to feel embarrassed. But then, later on, it occurred to me that maybe it wasn't that at all. Maybe *he* didn't want to be embarrassed about how unusual *his* house is, and how weird *his* parents are. I mean, it's not like they're the happiest couple in the world or anything, plus the whole Lutheran business, and Brian's dad being such a complimenter even with me. Not to mention that the guy *watches golf* for crying out loud. It wasn't that Brian thought his folks were better; actually, I think he thought they were worse.

Which has nothing to do with D-I basketball, except that it does. Because all season long, I've thought I wasn't good enough to play D-I. Sure, I could rattle off my stats and scoring and abilities — I knew *those* were good enough. But I never thought *I* was. But, just like I never took the time to see the world, to see me, from Brian's point of view, I never took the time to see the world from the coaches'. To realize that maybe they had more experience with recruiting than I did, duh, and that because they believed in me, maybe I should believe in myself.

Which is why I called. To acknowledge that I was scared, sure, but even so I might be willing to go for it. To try at least to be the player I believed now that I could become, that the U of M already saw in me. The player that Darey and I could become together.

I asked Coach K if I could use his office for a minute, and he said okay, and right quick before I changed my mind I dialed. I wasn't sure what I was going to say actually, except that I was sorry for calling on a Friday night even though she had said to call whenever.

"Hey there, D.J.," the coach said right off when I introduced myself. "How are you doing?"

"Great. We just won a game. Against our, you know, ri-
vals . . ." I took a deep breath. "Um. I'm, um . . . I'm thinking
about verbaling."

"That's fantastic!" There was a little pause. "You do mean
with us, don't you?"

Which got me grinning. "Yeah. I mean with you."

"You don't seem completely set on it, though."

"Yeah. It's a huge deal, Big Ten ball."

"It is. You're still thinking about the Wisconsin game,
aren't you? I worried about that."

Oh, it was cool she knew that. "Yeah. Tyrona."

"That was tough. I won't deny it. It takes time to recover
from something like that. Even though it's part of the game,
it still stinks."

"It's just I'm worried, you know. I'm worried I'll screw
up." All of a sudden my voice cracked. I was almost crying.

"You know, D.J., there's not a girl I've recruited who wasn't
scared, only most of them are too stubborn to admit it.
Frankly, I'd be a lot more concerned if you weren't worried."

I swallowed. "Guess you've got nothing to worry about
then."

She laughed. "You think it's stressful now, just wait until
you start coaching."

"Great. Just when I thought I had something to look forward to." But I smiled when I said it.

"D.J., I couldn't be happier about this. You'll be a just fantastic asset to our team, I know you will. And you know you're free to tell anyone you want, your local paper or —"

"*What?*" Which was extremely rude of me, but I think you know by now how I feel about the entire news business industry.

"Or not!" the coach laughed. "It's totally up to you. The point is, *we* can't tell anyone, not until you sign a letter of intent next November. Then we'll put together a press release, hold a news conference . . ."

"Oh, great." Which was sarcastic, you know, the way I said it. But it also wasn't.

So we chatted a bit more about the other eight billion NCAA rules I needed to know, how I could change my mind but she sure hoped I wouldn't (which she didn't say out loud because I guess that's against one of the rules, but it came through in her voice loud and clear). Then I got off the phone and went out to the lobby, where Mom and Dad and Win and Coach K and a bunch of other families were waiting, and when Mom asked what took me so long, I said I'd just called Minnesota to verbal.

All the stress of that phone call — of the whole last two months — all that stress was totally paid back, just by the look on Win's face.

"You called? Just now?" he asked, almost jumping out of his wheelchair, he was so upset. "Without . . . without . . ."

"Without you," Mom finished, patting him on the arm. "D.J., that's wonderful."

"Congratulations, sport," Dad said, catching me up in a huge bear hug. And Coach K hugged me, and the parents and girls, and Win even managed after a couple minutes to stop choking himself and grunt that the U of M might be okay even though I hadn't looked at many other schools, and I could have waited a *little* bit more. Which was especially rich coming from him, but at least the guy was trying.

I called Brian Saturday morning to tell *him,* and he said he'd always known I'd pick Minnesota but he couldn't help but hope. And he said he'd definitely be there every time I played Madison, and that maybe tonight we should, you know, go out together. To celebrate.

Only when he went to tell his mom, let her know he was going out and everything — I love this so much because it's such a relief when other kids' folks are mortifying — she really put the screws in him. Because apparently Mrs. Nelson and my mom had run into each other at the Super Saver and while they were chatting and Mom was thanking her for the Christmas decorations and everything, she let slip about our big trip to Mall of America and how beautiful (her word) I looked in my dress. And so when Brian told Mrs. Nelson the two of us were going out, she said in that way moms have that is more ordering than suggesting that it would be awfully nice if he treated it like a real date and we both got dressed up.

And you know what? Brian actually went for it. He actually seemed kind of into it. I couldn't tell if it was his Oprah Winfrey mom or just because he's such a good guy. I didn't mind either, to tell you the truth. I guess I like that dress more than I thought, getting to wear my b-ball earrings and all. Brian looked pretty nice too, with this sweater, and shoes that were shiny black and very much the opposite of tennies, although he said they're surprisingly comfortable, which I have to believe because why would anyone lie about a thing like that.

Dad even got a little teary seeing us, which was weird, and he made this big deal of trying to find the camera so Mom could have a picture because she'd left that afternoon with Win, heading back to Minnesota. But of course he couldn't, so he ended up taking a picture with Brian's cell phone and Brian promised to e-mail it to her.

We went out for pizza — real exciting, I know, but what can you do. It was either that or the Alpenhaus. It was mostly families eating seeing as it was still pretty early, the little kids bouncing around the way they do in restaurants. I told Brian Amber's meatballi story, and he agreed that meatballi was such a better term than meatballs and that he was never again going to call them anything else.

And then Amber and Dale walked in.

Dale caught sight of us and came right over, which of course she would, pulling off her hat and her big coat like she was settling in forever.

Well, I just about died. Amber's never been a big fan of Brian, for one thing. Plus I'd never really explained to Brian about her and Dale. I mean, he's got a gay cousin in Chicago and all, but it's different when you're in high school in middle-of-nowhere Wisconsin.

But. But Brian was my friend, and Amber and Dale were my friends, and I needed to stop being such a baby. If I could play D-I ball, I could at least for once act like a freaking grownup. "Um, hey," I managed. "You . . . want to join us?"

Dale immediately plopped down next to Brian, introducing herself and saying they could stay for a few minutes, while Amber squeezed in beside me. She took a long look at my dress.

"It's silly, I know . . ." I said. Trying, you know, to cut her off.

"No, it's not. It looks real pretty on you. Makes you look all straight."

"Oh. Um, thanks." Because I think this was a compliment. Plus she said it was a really good color, which is actually something she's great at, colors and stuff, even if the combinations aren't the sort of things Mom would choose.

So Amber and I chatted away while Dale told Brian all the best restaurants in Milwaukee, and he acted like this was the best information he'd ever heard in his life. Then the pizza guy shouted something and Dale hopped up because they were just there for takeout, because Dale had a friend visiting who's a vegetarian so they were picking up a couple veggie pizzas. Which sounded like a total waste of money to me, but Brian asked to see them and said they smelled so good that he was going to order one too.

Looking at Dale, I couldn't help thinking that she could get along with anyone. All those tough barbecue guys, Brian, my dad . . . No matter who it is or how much you'd think that person wouldn't be so into a *lesbian*, she makes it fine. And it occurred to me that the reason she makes it work, probably, is because she's so comfortable with herself. And you know, that's not such a bad notion, in the whole life-lesson business. Being comfortable with yourself. Because if you're not okay with who you are, why should anyone else be?

Later on, after Dale and Amber left and our food came — that's one thing I can say about being non-size-zero; it sure makes it fun to eat — the door banged open and a bunch of Hawley guys came pounding in.

Seeing them, it was like every stomach butterfly I've ever had in my life showed up all at once. Only the butterflies were the size of vultures.

From the look on Brian's face, he was getting major butterflies too. He glanced at me and you could just see him trying not to be nervous.

"I've got two words for you," I said. (Okay, I admit this was really mean of me. But I couldn't help it.) "Club football."

"Ha ha." He took a deep breath and cleared his throat. "Yo, dudes. Over here."

The guys looked our way, and I could see them doing a double take, eyeing each other kind of sideways as they piled into the booths near ours, saying hey to Brian and punching his shoulder.

One of them held his hand out to me. "Hey. I'm Carl Dietz. Tyler's cousin? Congratulations, man." He turned to the guys around him. "She just got offered a free ride to Minnesota. As a junior."

"Yeah," said one of the other guys in this real snotty voice. "For *girls'* basketball."

Well, you should have seen the reaction to *that.* All the guys went "Oooooo" the way you do when someone's just been dissed, and started grinning like crazy at each other, and Brian said to the guy, really coolly, "You want to take her on? One on one?"

"Wait — hey — that's not what I meant —"

"How about you, D.J.?" Brian turned to me. "You up for it?"

I shrugged. "I wouldn't want to bruise my hands." Which was a line I learned from Aaron, just so you know, but I don't think he'd mind my using it.

Well, this cracked everyone up, and a couple guys slapped palms with me and really started putting it to that anti-girls'-b-ball guy, who kept trying to explain what he'd meant but of course there's no way he could have meant anything other than what he said. Then someone else asked how my brother was doing.

"He's doing okay," I said. Because he was. Now that I'd verbaled, he was going to have to find a new bone to chew on. Knowing Win, though, that wasn't going be too hard.

"You should hear my dad," the guy said. "Whenever we complain the least little bit, he's all like, 'You think Win Schwenk is whining right now? Get off your butts and go shovel!'"

"Tell me about it," another guy said.

They all laughed, nodding at this . . . and you know what? All of a sudden I realized my stomach butterflies had flown away. Every last one.

So. Meeting Brian's gang . . . that was pretty trippy. Finding out that those guys are normal, more or less. As normal as the rest of us, anyway. That was okay.

And there's one more guy I should probably mention. Remember when Kathy Ott drove me to Minneapolis to visit the U of M, way back when? And the whole way there she was chatting away? Well, one of the things she told me was how much Win appreciated everything I'd done for him. Apparently he'd called one night and had a long talk with Jimmy Ott about it. He even said — according to Kathy, who's not the kind of person to make stuff like this up — Win said I'd saved his life.

Which you have to admit is a pretty strange way to hear that, you know, through your ex-boyfriend's high school football coach's wife.

At the time I was pretty angry about the whole thing. That my own brother couldn't even say "You saved my life" to my face. Because I've thought it myself more than once, you know, those exact words, and to hear them from Win would have been . . . it would have a been a boost. It would have meant the world to me. And the fact he couldn't say them aloud, even to his *lifesaver* . . . well, that didn't make me so happy. It made me even more ticked off at him than I usually am.

But I've thought a lot since then, about what Kathy said and what Win didn't. Of course, for one thing there's the whole truth that Schwenks can't talk. I mean, look how bad we are even with little issues; no wonder he couldn't bring up something as big as that, bring it up to my face and all. Finally, after I'd thought about this and chewed on it for weeks and weeks, in between all those other big subjects I was chewing on, it occurred to me that maybe his riding me these past months, hassling me about scholarships and videotapes, his insistence that I play D-I, the way he called all those coaches himself with his special SCI phone and typed his way to all those websites . . . maybe that was his way of demonstrating gratitude.

Well, if that was his screwed-up Schwenk way of showing gratitude, I was just as Schwenk-awful at receiving it. Sheesh. But no matter how angry I've been these past months, and resentful, and phone-slamming, I-won't-talk-to-him mad, that doesn't mean I don't know what he did.

Win, you say I saved your life. Well, you didn't save mine: you got me one. You've found me a better life than I ever imagined I deserved. And no matter how much I refused to listen, and kept shouting out that you were wrong, you kept insisting I was worth it. Until I had no alternative left but to hear you out.

I'll never forget that. Never. And just so you know, I will think of you . . . well, I'll think of you a lot. Every Big Ten game I play, every time I sit there waiting to run out in front of ten thousand people and play the very best I can, to be the very best player that D.J. Schwenk could ever be, I will think of you, Win, and this is what I will whisper to myself:

Thank you.

ACKNOWLEDGMENTS

Tight end Bennie Cunningham played for Clemson University and then the Pittsburgh Steelers, competing in two Super Bowls. He now works in the Guidance Department of West-Oak High School in South Carolina, and has graciously offered the use of his name to a Schwenk Farm cow.

Aaron's cheesehead hat was inspired by a gift from the charming students and staff of Cherokee Heights Middle School in Madison, Wisconsin. I apologize to them and to the hundreds of readers from all over the world who have asked (often quite forcefully) when I was going to get around to finishing this book. I know it's taken far too long, and I hope it meets your expectations.

Becky Bohm, Barb Smith, Ted Riverso and the incomparable Patsy Kahmann of the University of Minnesota patiently answered my many basketball questions, and then patiently answered them again. Sylvia Hatchell's *Complete Guide to Coaching Girls' Basketball* taught me pretty much everything D.J. now knows about the game.

Though Stewart Irving and I were both raised in Connecticut, he had the great good luck to end up at Berkeley, where in 1990 he introduced me to They Might Be Giants and *Flood*. "Dead" remains a lifelong favorite, and Stewart a good friend. Every couple of years we call each other and marvel at the fact we've somehow turned into grownups.

Liz, Mom, Dad, Nick, Nick, Mimi, Mari: thanks for reading, for listening, for critiquing, for laughing. Jill Grinberg took the tangle of the first FAC draft and shaped it into a narrative thread; Margaret Raymo coaxed me into weaving this thread into something worth reading. I cannot image a more supportive and perceptive agent or editor.

My Wisconsin cousin Forrest Olson was a high school and college basketball star. I remember in particular an August reunion when I offered to jog with him around the lake, and his father whispered later that I'd almost killed him: apparently distance running hadn't been part of his off-season training regimen. This experience and several others, I now realize, formed the nucleus of *Dairy Queen*. After a heroic battle with cancer, Forrest passed away in 2007. Yet even in their grief, his widow and parents have found time to explain team sports, clarify Vikings-Packers enmity, and identify innumerable errors, large and small, in my drafts. *Front and Center* is a story about courage and perseverance; Darla, Carol, and Rod embody these virtues.

And finally, I thank James. You are, in the very best possible sense, my Brian.